Education in Sexuality

Mary Bronson Merki, Ph.D.

McGraw-Hill

New York, New York   Columbus, Ohio   Mission Hills, California   Peoria, Illinois

Photo Credits

Cover, © John Terence Turner/FPG International;

1, Mak-I Photo Design; 3, file photo; 5, Doug Martin; 8, Aaron Haupt; 11, Aaron Haupt; 13, Mak-I Photo Design; 14, Aaron Haupt; 15, Doug Martin; 18, Mak-I Photo Design; 20, John Walsh/Science Photo Library/Photo Researchers, Inc.; 27, Lennart Nilsson/The Incredible Machine/National Geographic Society; 34, Aaron Haupt; 36, Mak-I Photo Design; 38, file photo; 42, Mak-I Photo Design; 44, Mak-I Photo Design; 45, Doug Martin; 47, Mak-I Photo Design; 50, Mak-I Photo Design; 52, Doug Martin; 53, Mak-I Photo Design/MI Schottenstein Homes, Inc.; 56, Paul Von Stroheim/Plessner/The Stock Shop, Inc.; 57, Aaron Haupt; 60, Doug Martin; 62, © Vladimir Lange/The Image Bank; 63, Aaron Haupt; 64, Andy Levin/Photo Researchers, Inc.; 67, (bl) Lennart Nilsson/Behold Man/Little, Brown and Company; 67, (br) Lennart Nilsson/The Incredible Machine/National Geographic Society; 67, (c) Lennart Nilsson/The Incredible Machine/National Geographic Society; 67, (t) Lennart Nilsson/The Incredible Machine/National Geographic Society; 68, Doug Martin; 70, Peter J. Kaplan/The Stock Shop/Medichrome; 71, Doug Martin; 74, Doug Martin/MI Schottenstein Homes, Inc.; 76, Aaron Haupt/Campaign For Our Children, Inc., Baltimore, Maryland; 79, Lee White Photography; 80, © Sal DiMarco, Black Star; 81, Aaron Haupt; 86, file photo; 87, AP/Wide World Photos; 87, AP/Wide World Photos; 90, Mak-I Photo Design/MI Schottenstein Homes, Inc.; 93, file photo; 95, Custom Medical Stock; 98, file photo; 100, (b) © Centers for Disease Control, Atlanta, Georgia; 100, (t) Aaron Haupt; 103, Mak-I Photo Design/MI Schottenstein Homes, Inc.; 105, file photo; 106, file photo; 109, file photo

Illustrator
Nancy Heim

Send all inquiries to:
Glencoe/McGraw-Hill
15319 Chatsworth Street
P.O. Box 9609
Mission Hills, California 91346-9609

ISBN: 0-02-651504-0 (Student Text)
ISBN: 0-02-651505-9 (Teacher's Annotated Edition)

Printed in the United States of America.

3 4 5 6 7 8 9 POH 01 00 99 98 97

C O N T E N T S

C O N T E N T S

CHAPTER

1

SEXUALITY AND YOU

LESSON 1
Sexuality and Decision Making

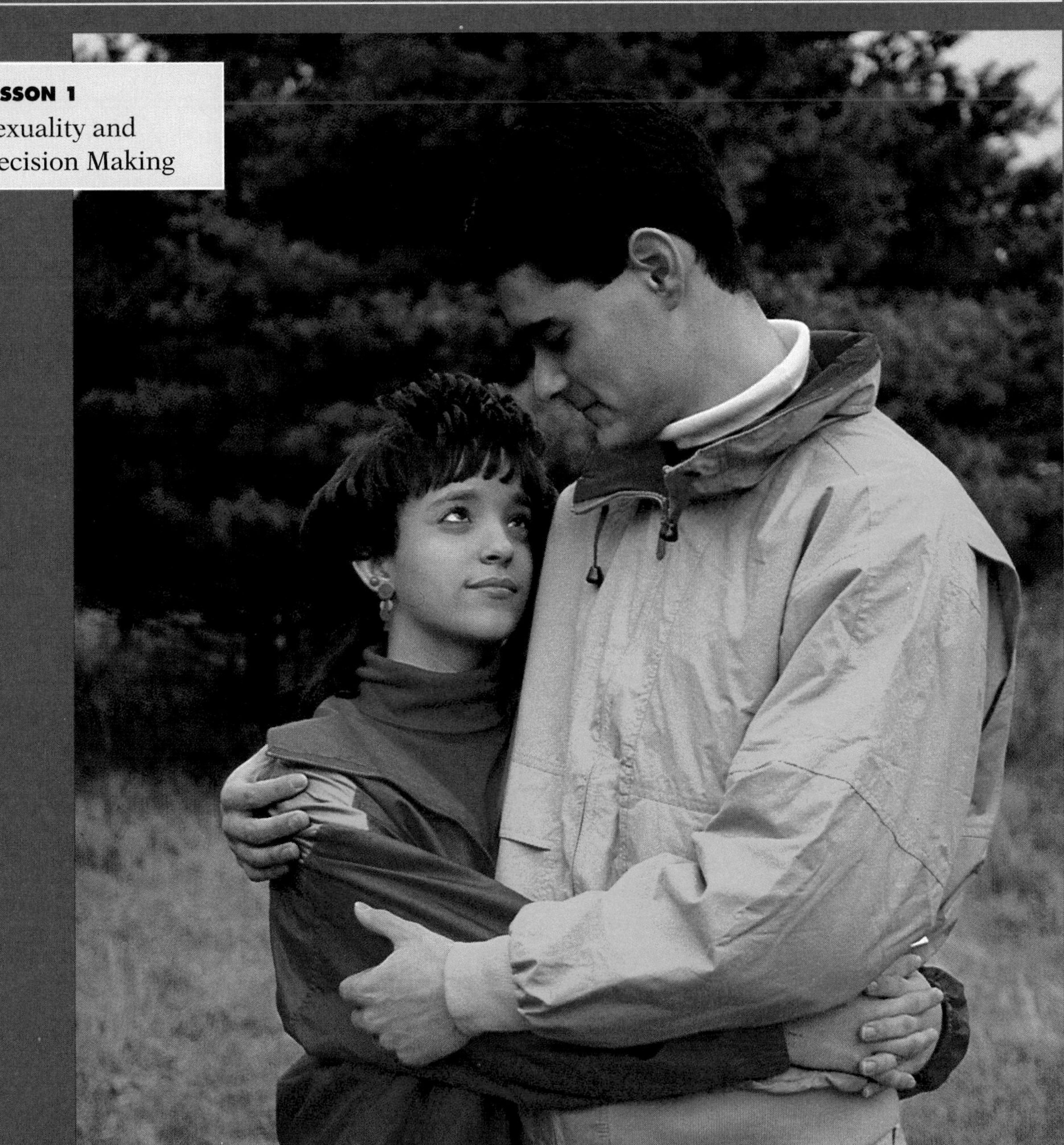

LESSON 1

Sexuality and Decision Making

LESSON 1 FOCUS

Terms to Use

- Self-concept
- Goal setting
- Sexuality

Concepts to Learn

- Your self-concept relates to your ability to make healthy choices.
- Goal setting helps you make responsible decisions that promote your health.
- Your sexuality includes the way you act, your personality, and your feelings about yourself because you are male or female.
- Everyone has a need for love and personal value.

Sex—just saying the word can bring laughter to some and images to others. A lot of people think about it. Some people talk about it. A lot of information has been written about it. Advertisers often try to use it to their advantage. Think of the ads you have seen in magazines or on television. Sex is a common theme used to help sell products. Consider these messages in ads:

- "Wearing this perfume will drive them crazy."
- "Using this mouthwash will guarantee you that date."
- "You'll be irresistible after using this shampoo."
- "Wearing our jeans will make you stand out in the crowd."

Millions of dollars are spent on such advertising. Companies want you to buy their products, and they know how to get your attention. The media glamorizes physical appearance and stresses that to be sexy a person needs to be popular, beautiful, and successful. Promoting sex sells products.

Even though information or promotion of sex seems to be everywhere, some people may not feel comfortable talking about it. Sex, to them, is a private matter. Some people may not know much about sex or like to ask questions about it. Other people may only have information from what they hear from friends or others they know. Some of this information may not be correct.

It's important to have factual information about sex. Factual information will not only help you understand your growth and development but also help you form attitudes to make decisions that promote your health and prevent some diseases and premature death.

Your Sexuality and Health

Your **sexuality** refers to everything about you as a male or female person. It includes the way you act, your personality, and your feelings about yourself because you are male or female. Learning about sexuality is an ongoing process. The messages you received while growing up and your observations of those around you made up part of that learning. Your personal experiences and feelings also play a part in the development of your sexuality.

Your sexuality relates to your total health. Your total health includes physical, mental, and social aspects of health.

Physical Health

Physical health means that all parts and systems of the body work well together. It means that your body has the ability to withstand the stresses of normal daily life. It means having strength and energy to pursue physical, mental, emotional, and social challenges and changes.

Physical health, as related to your sexuality, includes practicing good health care of your reproductive system. It also includes having regular physical exams and making decisions that protect your reproductive system. This involves preventing unwanted pregnancy and sexually transmitted diseases, including the virus known to cause AIDS.

Mental Health

Mental health includes how you like, accept, and feel about yourself; how well you relate to others; and how you meet the demands of daily life. A person with good mental health is in touch with his or her emotions and expresses them in acceptable, healthful ways. Such an individual can usually deal with the problems and frustrations of life without being overwhelmed by them.

Mental health also calls for a person to use his or her mind to develop thinking skills. People with good mental health enjoy learning and know that striving for information and understanding can be an exciting, lifelong process.

Handling emotions in positive ways is a part of mental health. As human beings, we all have two basic emotional needs. First, we each have a need for love and belonging. We are social beings, so we need other people. We need to feel that we belong to, and are a valued member of, a group. We each have a need to love and be loved.

The second emotional need we all have is to feel that we have personal value or worth. We have a need to achieve, to make a contribution, and to be recognized. This is such a strong need that some people will seek negative attention for recognition.

Self-concept is the mental image you have about yourself. It is your unique set of perceptions, ideas, and attitudes about yourself. Your self-concept began to form as soon as you were born. You received messages from people around you. These messages—especially from people who are important to you—helped to form your self-concept. Your self-concept is probably the single most important factor influencing what you do. Your self-concept relates to your ability to make healthy choices.

DID YOU KNOW?

Here are some healthy ways to meet your emotional needs.

- Focus on your strengths rather than on your weaknesses.
- Spend some time volunteering for people who need help—disabled children, older adults, or shut-ins. Doing something for someone who is in need can help you feel good about yourself.

Mental health includes how you relate to others and meet the demands of life.

The messages you receive from others help form your self-concept.

Poor self-concept seems to relate directly to unhealthy choices. People who like themselves are more likely to take better care of themselves than people with low self-concepts.

People with high self-concepts find healthy ways to meet their emotional needs. However, consider a young person who is struggling to understand his or her emerging sexuality and does not feel anyone loves him or her. Such a person might try to meet the need to be loved by getting involved in unhealthy, often sexual, relationships. Some may get pregnant, thinking that a baby will provide a source of love. As you learn more about sexuality and making responsible decisions, you will learn ways to meet your emotional needs and promote your health and sexuality.

Mental health, as related to your sexuality, includes learning to communicate effectively and to express, understand, and handle sexual feelings. A healthy sexuality also includes learning more about yourself and improving your self-concept.

HEALTH UPDATE

LOOKING AT TECHNOLOGY

Differences Between the Sexes

Most little boys prefer to play with cars, trucks, and building blocks. Most little girls prefer to play with dolls and kitchen toys. Though many people may have believed these differences were the result of how children were raised, researchers have observed and discovered that these preferences may, in fact, be the result of distinct differences in the male and female brain. This may explain the reason that despite more equal opportunities for males and females, gender differences and preferences still exist.

What possible explanations could account for gender-linked differences? A few possibilities include the following:

- An area in the hypothalamus is larger in males than in females. This can result in more aggressive behavior and increased sexual desire in males than in females.
- A part of the brain that connects the brain's right and left hemispheres may be larger in females than in males. This would increase a female's ability to read emotional clues. Females also use both sides of their brain and do better with verbal tasks.
- This smaller connection between the two hemispheres helps males perform better with visual-spatial tasks, like reading a map.

Both genders have differences, but we all are also unique. Varying levels of hormones account for different interests and abilities regardless of gender. For example, the best math student in your class may be female, despite the fact that males generally perform better in math.

Both genders can develop in their areas of difference. In the last 15 years, gender differences have dropped on test scores for verbal and math skills. This may have resulted because of changes in family, societal, and educational processes.

Social health includes developing a variety of relationships.

Social Health

Social health involves the way you get along with others. It includes your ability to make and keep friends and to work and play in cooperative ways, seeking and lending support when necessary. It involves communicating well and sharing your feelings with others. Social health, as related to your sexuality, includes meeting new people, dating, and developing a variety of relationships.

A Decision-Making Model

Decisions, especially about your health and sexuality, can be difficult to make. When you are confronted with a tough decision, break down the decision to be made into smaller, more manageable steps.

1. **State the situation that requires a decision.** Be sure you have a firm grasp on the problem. This sounds easy, but in fact many people find this to be the most difficult step.
2. **List possible choices.** Think of as many different ways of solving the problem as you can. Enlist the help of a parent or other adult in listing the alternatives.
3. **Consider the consequences and your values—personal, family, religious, and legal.** Ask yourself in each case what negative and positive results would occur if that particular choice were made. Again, seek the help of an adult.
4. **Make a decision based on everything you know at this point and act on it.** Use everything you know at this point to make a decision. Once you have made the decision, you need to take action.
5. **Evaluate your decision.** Determine if your choice was a good one. If not, return to your list of possible choices and try again. Or learn from your mistakes and be ready to deal with a similar situation in the future.

Of course, you will not use such a detailed process every time you need to make a decision or are faced with a choice. However, you might find it helpful to practice this process on easier problems. Then, when faced with more difficult decisions, you will be better prepared.

DID YOU KNOW?

- Sexuality education classes were probably not taught to your parents. So some parents may have few examples of how to discuss sex with their teens. In addition, some parents are not comfortable discussing the topic of sex. It is even more difficult to begin talking to a teenager if such discussions have never before taken place. Remember, communication is a two-way street. If you don't try to respond to a parent's efforts to talk about sex, the conversation will not be successful.

One of the most important points to remember in the decision-making process is that you are the one responsible for your choices. If you have examined the consequences before deciding, you should not have a list of excuses when someone asks you about your actions.

Each of us makes very important decisions. It's important to consider if and how your choices will affect your health. Making good decisions is a skill that can be learned, though like most skills, decision making needs to be practiced. Remember, having a good self-concept helps you make healthy decisions.

Goal Setting and Healthy Decisions

Goal setting is part of making decisions. **Goal setting** involves making decisions that will help you meet a goal you have in mind. The following steps will help you reach your goal.

1. **Decide on one area on which you want to work.** Make your goal realistic, something you can attain.
2. **List what you will do to reach your goal.** Identify others who can help you and support your efforts.
3. **Give yourself an identified period of time to reach your goal.** Build in several checkpoints to evaluate how you are doing.
4. **State a reward for yourself for achieving your goal.**

Having a good self-concept promotes goal setting. If you feel good about yourself, you are not afraid to set goals or try to reach those goals.

As a teenager you will be faced with decisions that deal not only with your health but also dating, relationships, and sexuality. Your decisions will affect you, your family, and your future. Making good decisions is a skill that can be learned. Having a good self-concept and setting goals can help you make responsible decisions. Making responsible decisions is a key to maintaining a high level of health.

LESSON 1 REVIEW

Reviewing Facts and Vocabulary

1. Define *self-concept* and explain how it relates to your decisions about health.
2. What is the first step in reaching a goal?
3. Define *sexuality,* and discuss how it is developed.
4. What three areas make up total health?
5. Name the two basic emotional needs that are important to all human beings.

Thinking Critically

6. **Synthesis.** How can a poor self-concept affect decision making? Give two examples.
7. **Synthesis.** What are some of the negative consequences of having too much sexually explicit material in advertisements?
8. **Evaluation.** Why do you think it is difficult for teenagers to discuss sex with adults?

Applying Health Knowledge

9. Design one magazine advertisement and write an outline for a television commercial to sell each of the following products without using sexual images: designer jeans, perfume, and a sporting event.

CHAPTER 1

REVIEW

Reviewing Facts and Vocabulary

1. Why is it important to have factual information about sex?
2. Explain the three areas of health and give one example of a decision that could affect your total health in a positive way.
3. Name the five steps in the decision-making process.
4. What is self-concept?
5. List the goal-setting steps.
6. What does your sexuality include?

Thinking Critically

7. **Synthesis.** Write a paragraph explaining from whom facts about sex should come.
8. **Synthesis.** Give a specific example of a choice that could affect your physical, mental, and social well-being.
9. **Synthesis.** List ten specifics from your environment that can influence the development of your sexuality.
10. **Analysis.** Write five positive outcomes of choosing not to engage in sexual activity.
11. **Synthesis.** What might be consequences of engaging in sexual activity to satisfy emotional needs?

Applying Health Knowledge

12. For one day, keep a journal and make notes throughout the day on how you are feeling about yourself. Try to identify specific ways you tried to meet emotional needs. Evaluate your findings. What was happening when you felt good about yourself? What was happening when you weren't feeling too good about yourself? How did you deal with positive and negative feelings?
13. Describe some components of traditional sex roles. What were males supposed to be like? How about females? List ways that these roles have changed in recent years.
14. Select a magazine ad that uses sex to sell its product. Analyze the ad. What are the messages? How are they misleading?
15. Imagine that you write an advice column for the local newspaper. What advice could you give to a reader who wrote in and said she is engaging in sexual activity with her boyfriend even though she feels it is not a good idea?

Beyond the Classroom

16. **Parental Involvement.** With your parents' or another family member's help, use the five-step decision-making process to make a decision in the following situation: Nick has asked Carrie to go to the school dance with him. Carrie is reluctant to go because she has heard that Nick had sex with another girl. Nick is very popular and Carrie realizes that this could help her socially if she does go with Nick. What should she do in this situation?
17. **Community Involvement.** Visit the closest Public Assistance agency in your community. Find out how many unwed, teenage mothers in your city are receiving public assistance and how many of those have dropped out of school. Write a paper suggesting some goals these mothers might set to improve the situation for themselves and their children. What might you do to help?
18. **Community Involvement.** Survey five people of different ages. Ask them what self-concept means to them. Compare your findings with other members of your class.
19. **Parental Involvement.** Ask a parent or other adult at home to tell you about an important decision he or she had to make as a teen. Find out the process the person used to make the decision and if he or she believes it was the right choice.

CHAPTER

2 Adolescence—A Time of Change

LESSON 1

ADOLESCENCE—DOOR TO ADULTHOOD

Think of all the changes that take place in the human body during adolescence. There are physical, mental, and social changes. There is perhaps no other time in our lives when we experience so many changes.

Everyone goes through this process in order to get to adulthood. Your parents went through the same changes you are experiencing. Ask them about their adolescent years. What were their questions, worries, or problems? Though you may face different situations than they did, you may be surprised to find that they shared some of the same concerns you now have.

LESSON 1 FOCUS

TERMS TO USE

- Developmental task
- Personal identity

CONCEPTS TO LEARN

- There are nine developmental tasks identified for adolescents.
- Personal identity involves the factors you believe make up the unique you.

Tasks of Adolescence

The period of adolescence has been carefully studied by psychologists and sociologists for over 50 years. These people have identified certain developmental tasks that can be considered basic to adolescence. A **developmental task** is something that needs to occur during a particular age period for a person to continue his or her growth toward becoming a healthy, mature adult.

Robert Havinghurst, a well-known sociologist who studies adolescence, suggests that there are nine such tasks worked on throughout the teen years and often into one's twenties. These tasks are listed as follows:

1. forming more mature relationships with peers of both sexes,
2. achieving a masculine or feminine social role,
3. accepting one's physique and using one's body effectively,
4. achieving emotional independence from parents and other adults,
5. preparing for marriage and family life,
6. preparing for a career,
7. acquiring a set of personal standards as a guide to behavior,
8. developing social intelligence, which includes becoming aware of human needs and becoming motivated to help others attain their goals,
9. developing conceptual and problem-solving skills.

As you can see, there is quite a lot involved in growing up and becoming a mature adult! Many of these tasks can be grouped under the general task of achieving a **personal identity,** the factors you believe make up the unique you. This task has a great impact on all of the other tasks and centers around one's self-concept. Questions like "Who am I?" and "What do I want to be as a person?" are common in this search for identity.

PERSONAL-IDENTITY QUIZ

Read each statement. Decide how closely each one describes you as you are now.

1. I have a picture in my mind of what kind of man/woman I want to be as an adult. (2)
2. I think through problems I face, looking at several possible solutions. (9)
3. I have one or two very close friends whom I can talk to about almost anything. (1)
4. I know of several jobs I would be good at as an adult. (6)
5. I am aware of the activities of some of the civic groups in my community. (8)
6. I have more adult discussions with my parents or other adults at home than I used to. (4)
7. I am concerned about national and world problems that are in the news today. (8)
8. I can list the four most important beliefs I have. (7)
9. I know of some of the qualities I would look for in a marriage partner. (5)
10. People who know me know I act in a way that supports what I believe in. (7)
11. I am usually comfortable with my behavior as a male or female in social settings. (2)
12. I can describe some ways my life-style would change if I were married and if I had children. (5)
13. I listen to other people's ideas, even though they may differ from my own. (9)
14. I usually have success in making male and female friends with my peers. (1)
15. I know and am able to accept my physical strengths and weaknesses. (3)
16. I do some things alone or with my friends that I used to do with my family. (4)
17. I have several interests I would consider pursuing as a career. (6)
18. I make choices that promote my overall health and well-being. (3)

Now look at the statements that do not describe you. After each statement is the number of the basic task it relates to. Which tasks do you need to work on?

DID YOU KNOW?

Responsibility means moral, legal, or mental accountability, reliability, and trustworthiness. What do you take responsibility for?

- Do you carry through with what you say you are going to do?
- Are you usually on time?
- Do you admit to the mistakes that you make?
- Do you try not to make the same mistakes repeatedly?
- When conflict arises, do you attempt to discuss rather than argue?
- Do you show consideration for other people's needs or concerns?

As you show that you can handle responsibility, you are likely to be given more.

Intellectual Development

Responsible decision making becomes a critical issue during adolescence. Certainly you made many decisions as a child. However, it is not so much making the decisions that we are talking about, but how they are made. During adolescence important cognitive (intellectual) development takes place. That is, you begin to learn higher-level thinking skills.

As a child, you were a concrete thinker. What you saw was what you believed existed. Consider showing a child two containers that are exactly the same size, but are different shapes. One is tall and thin, the other short and fat. The child is unlikely to understand that they are both the same size. Now, pour the same amount of water in each container. The child is likely to say that there is more water in the taller one because it is tall.

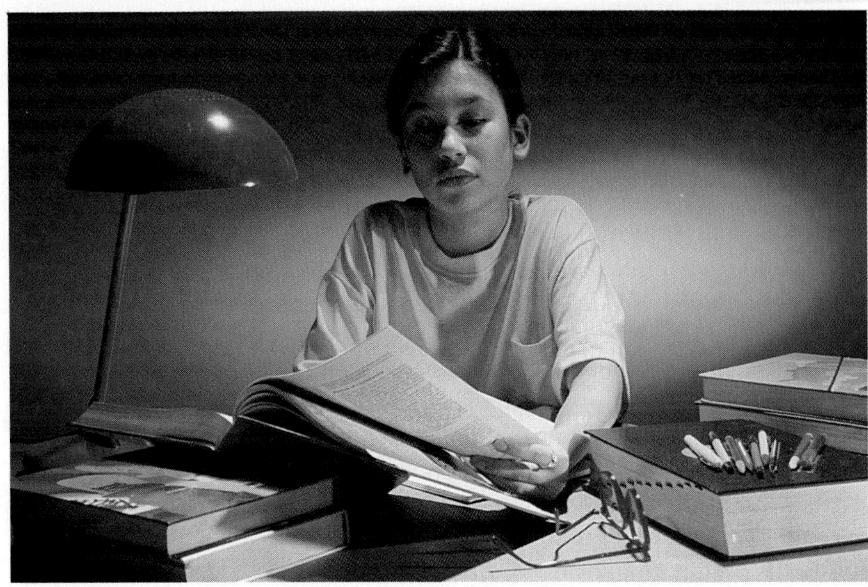

Your ability to think on a higher level increases in adolescence.

During adolescence you develop abstract thinking ability, that is, you are able to consider alternatives and examine consequences. You can better understand cause-and-effect relationships. If you were now shown the two containers of water, you would be able to reason that it looks like there is more in the tall glass but that, really, there is the same amount of water in both.

During adolescence, your ability to think logically—reason things out—increases. You can begin to solve more complicated problems. Your memory ability also increases. Your thinking becomes more flexible.

Remember, all of these changes do not just happen overnight. They develop over time. As you try out these new abilities, you are likely to make mistakes—everyone does. What is important is that you learn from those mistakes.

LESSON 1 REVIEW

Reviewing Facts and Vocabulary

1. Define *developmental task.*
2. Name four developmental tasks for adolescents suggested by sociologist Robert Havinghurst.
3. Discuss abstract thinking ability and tell during what stage it is usually developed.
4. During adolescence, does logical thinking increase or decrease? Explain your answer.

Thinking Critically

5. **Evaluation.** What problems might occur if a person developed friendships only with people of the same sex?
6. **Synthesis.** Explain why preparing for a career is an important developmental task for you to do now as a teenager.
7. **Synthesis.** How might your personal identity influence your standards and behaviors?

Applying Health Knowledge

8. Observe a younger brother, sister, or other relative between the ages of two and six. Take notes as they play and notice the type of activity in which they are engaged. From your observation, give an example of one concrete thinking skill that the child was performing.

LESSON 2

Changes During Adolescence

LESSON 2 FOCUS

Terms to Use

- Endocrine system
- Hormones
- Puberty
- Pituitary gland
- Gonads
- Testosterone (te•STAHS•tuh•rohn)
- Estrogen (ES•truh•juhn)
- Progesterone (proh•JES•tuh•rohn)

Concepts to Learn

- Hormones cause changes during adolescence.
- Everyone's timeline is different during puberty.
- Secondary sex characteristics occur during adolescence when sex hormones are produced.
- Sexual feelings result because of hormones in the body.

The body is complex and amazing. It is made up of a system of checks and balances. No one body system works independently of the others. The nervous system is the primary regulating system of the body. The **endocrine system** works closely with the nervous system in regulating body functions and is made up of ductless (tubeless) glands that secrete chemicals called hormones. **Hormones** are substances that regulate the activities of different body cells. Blood carries hormones to various parts of the body. These hormones also affect the autonomic nervous system, the system that helps the body maintain a stable environment. Just as in the case of the autonomic nervous system, you have no conscious control over your endocrine system.

The Function of Hormones

The word *hormone* means "to excite or set in motion." Hormones act as chemical regulators in three ways.

1. Hormones may stimulate a reaction in some other part of the body. For example, hormones work with the autonomic nervous system to stimulate the bodily activities needed in an emergency situation. Being frightened and feeling your heart rate increase is a physical change that occurs because of hormones. You do not have any control over the secretion of a hormone; that is, you cannot keep your heart rate from increasing when you are frightened. This is an important point to remember as you read about the changes that hormones cause in the body during adolescence.
2. Hormones play an important role during periods of growth by producing changes in body structures. These changes include bone development, maturation of the reproductive organs, and the development of secondary sex characteristics.
3. Hormones regulate the rate of body metabolism, the rate at which body cells produce energy.

Hormones play a major role during puberty. As you learn what happens and why, you may better understand the period of adolescence.

Puberty

Puberty is the period of growth from physical childhood to physical adulthood—a time when an individual becomes capable of reproduction. Puberty is characterized by rapid, uneven physical growth. Although most adolescents go through all the changes, each person's timeline is different. There is no other time in life when there is such a great variation in sizes and shapes of people who are the same age.

Such size variation can cause concern—especially for the person who is bigger or smaller than everyone else. It is important to know that everyone grows at a rate just right for them. The growth spurt during puberty depends largely on each individual's genetic inheritance. It appears to be controlled by the hypothalamus, a nerve center in the brain. Neurons from the hypothalamus stimulate the pituitary gland to release the hormone that results in body growth. The pituitary gland also releases other hormones that affect the brain, glands, skin, bones, muscles, and sex organs. These hormones also cause feelings and sensations never experienced before. The body begins to respond differently. It is important to understand these changes in order to be able to handle them appropriately.

DID YOU KNOW?

Everyone makes mistakes. As you begin making more decisions on your own, it is likely that some of the results of your decisions will not turn out as you planned. Or maybe you didn't really think through the decision before you acted. Now you are suffering the consequences. Maybe you are grounded, or perhaps someone is angry with you. Take some time to learn from this mistake. Ask yourself—and think:

- What could I have done differently?
- What might have happened if. . . (consider other alternatives)?

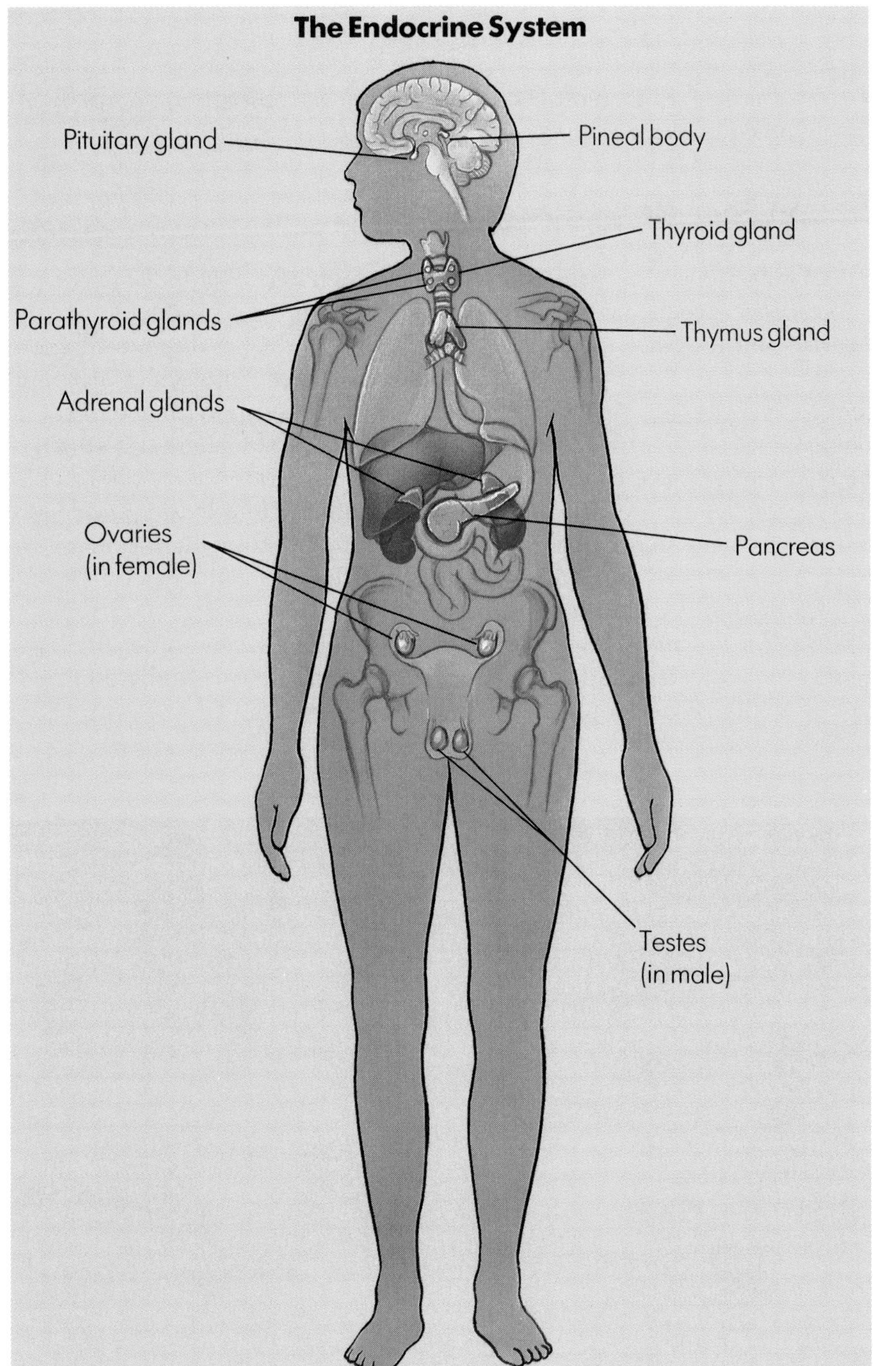

Hormones secreted by your endocrine glands cause many changes during adolescence.

DID YOU KNOW?

- There is nothing wrong with a high school student who isn't really interested in dating. Just as physical growth is very individual, so is social growth. Unfortunately, people are being pushed into social situations and dating at younger and younger ages, a time when they often are not ready for this type of social interaction. A person who is in high school and involved in school activities with his or her peers is very normal and is practicing healthy behaviors.

The Pituitary Gland

The master gland of the endocrine system is the **pituitary gland.** Its hormones regulate the growth rate and influence the action of the other glands. It is about the size of a pea and is located at the base of the brain.

The pituitary gland secretes two gonadotropic hormones that are responsible for the development of the gonads. **Gonads** is a term used to describe the reproductive organs, specifically the testes in the male and the ovaries in the female. The gonadotropic hormones are LH (luteinizing hormone) and FSH (follicle-stimulating hormone).

- In the male, LH controls the amount of testosterone produced. **Testosterone** is the sex hormone produced by the testes. FSH controls sperm production.
- In the female, FSH and LH control the levels of **estrogen** and **progesterone**—the two sex hormones produced by the ovaries.

Secondary Sex Characteristics

Secondary sex characteristics are those changes that occur during adolescence when progesterone and estrogen are produced by the ovaries and testosterone by the testes. Prior to the production of these sex hormones, there is little physical difference between males and females other than the type of genital organ present. With the onset of puberty, these similarities disappear. Secondary sex characteristics for males include broadened shoulders; facial, underarm, and pubic hair; deepened voice; increased muscular development; and longer and larger bones. Females experience breast development; underarm and pubic hair; and widened hips. Both males and females will experience the beginning of sexual desire.

Remember, everyone goes through these changes, but some will experience them earlier than others. These changes are very individual. For instance, breast development in females differs from person to person.

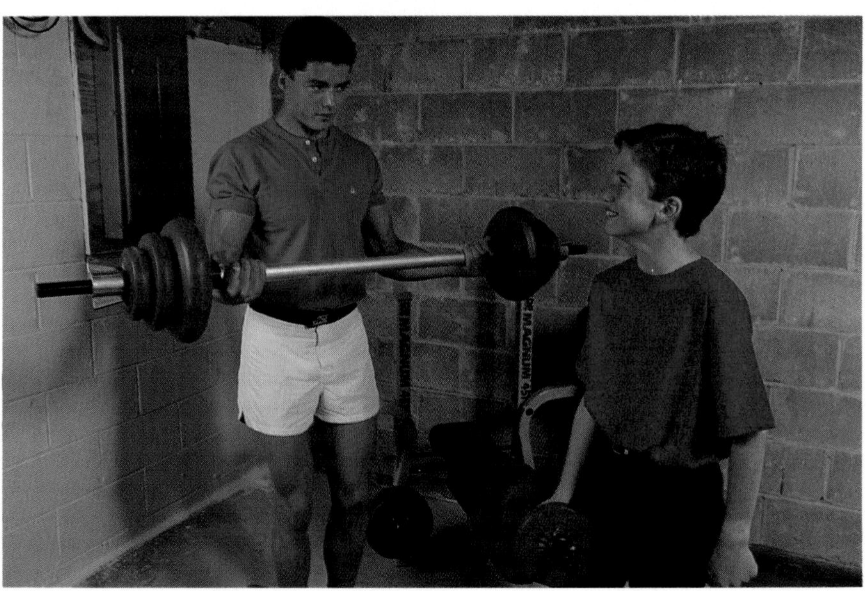

Secondary sex characteristics develop with the onset of puberty.

Breasts may not grow at the same rate or evenly. This means that one breast will likely be smaller, perhaps even shaped a little differently than the other. Such variations are perfectly normal. The size of a female's breasts is an inherited characteristic—something she cannot control. The size of the female's breasts has nothing to do with what kind of person she is.

The sex hormones released during puberty cause the oil and sweat glands in the body to become more active. This is one of the reasons acne becomes a problem during adolescence. As the sweat glands become more active, body odor can become a problem. Cleanliness and good health habits become more important than they were in the past.

During adolescence, most teens notice the opposite sex.

HEALTH UPDATE

LOOKING AT THE ISSUES

Looking Good

One of the developmental tasks of adolescence is to accept one's physique and use one's body effectively. Looking good is very important in our society and there is a lot of pressure to do so, especially during the teenage years. Our appearance plays a major role in how we view ourselves and how others view us. Our society views fitness, appearance, and good looks as the measure of a person's worth. The media has shown that slim but fit is the ideal we all should strive for. As a result, many Americans spend a lot of money on diets, beauty and fitness aids, and plastic surgery in an attempt to meet this ideal.

Analyzing Different Viewpoints

ONE VIEW. Looks are important in our society. We all should continuously strive to meet the goals of good looks set forth by our society.

A SECOND VIEW. What is inside a person is what counts. You could miss out on a terrific friendship if you chose only good-looking friends.

A THIRD VIEW. Working hard and doing a good job are more important than beauty, and people who are smart realize this.

A FOURTH VIEW. Looks are based on how much money a person chooses to spend on him- or herself.

A FIFTH VIEW. Society is placing a huge burden on people to fit a certain body image. Eating disorders can result from this pressure.

Exploring Your Views

1. Why do you think our society places such an emphasis on looking good?
2. How does this make you feel?
3. What situations have you seen where someone who was judged to be good-looking was shown favoritism?
4. How would you respond to a boss who shows favoritism to a person judged to be good-looking?

Sexual Feelings

The sex hormones also cause sexual feelings. It is important to understand why these feelings occur, because they may cause some confusion. It is important to remember that these feelings are normal and healthy. They will be with us throughout our adult lives.

The sex hormones cause the body to begin to respond to sexual stimulation. Such stimulation could be looking at a picture or a movie scene, holding hands, kissing—almost anything in our environment. The body responds to this stimulation—the face gets hot and flushed, the heart beats faster, the hands get clammy, and there is a fluttery feeling inside. We cannot keep this response from happening. It is normal. However, we can and must decide what to do about it. The response does not have to be acted upon. This is an important point to keep in mind.

Managing Sexual Feelings. Sexual responses in the body should not be confused with love. You may have heard people say, "I've never felt this way before," "He or she really turns me on," or "I must be in love." These physical feelings of excitement have nothing to do with being in love. Nor do they occur because he or she is "that special person." The feelings come about because of hormones in the body.

If you know what sexual feelings are, you can make more responsible decisions concerning them. It is easier to decide early about what you want for yourself before you are in a situation where these feelings have built up. At the appropriate time, talk about your feelings with your boyfriend or girlfriend. Talking about your feelings and your decisions helps you both know and understand what each of you want from your relationship.

LESSON 2 REVIEW

Reviewing Facts and Vocabulary

1. Name three ways in which hormones act as chemical regulators.
2. Explain why the rate of development during puberty is varied among teenagers.
3. Discuss the functions of the pituitary gland.
4. List the gonads found in males and those found in females.

Thinking Critically

5. **Synthesis.** How might the development of secondary sex characteristics affect an adolescent's social and emotional development?
6. **Analysis.** Compare the secondary sex characteristics that develop during puberty for males with those that females experience.

Applying Health Knowledge

7. Find out more about the nervous system, the autonomic nervous system, or the endocrine system. Choose one system to research and present a report to your class. Interview a doctor who specializes in the system you have chosen.
8. What would you say to your younger sister who asks you about differences in growth rate among your group of friends?

CHAPTER 2

REVIEW

Reviewing Facts and Vocabulary

1. Give an example of a physical change that might occur during adolescence.
2. Name the two gonadotropic hormones secreted by the pituitary gland.
3. Questions like "Who am I?" and "What do I want to be?" both relate to achieving what?
4. Being able to imagine involves what kind of thinking skill?
5. Do changes during puberty occur very rapidly or do they develop over time? Explain your answer.
6. The rate at which body cells produce energy is called what?
7. Name the developmental stage that occurs before adolescence and the stage that occurs after adolescence.
8. Growth spurts appear to be controlled by what nerve center in the brain?
9. What is the master gland of the endocrine system, and where is it located?
10. Name three secondary sex characteristics that occur in males and three that occur in females.
11. Identify the male gonads and the female gonads.
12. What mainly determines the size of a female's breasts?
13. Describe physical changes that occur when the body is responding to sexual stimulation.
14. Are sexual feelings and love the same thing? Explain your answer.

Thinking Critically

15. **Synthesis.** Give an example of something you can do to succeed in all nine of Robert Havinghurst's developmental tasks. Give an example for each task.
16. **Evaluation.** What might you say to help a friend who has poor self-esteem and is feeling depressed because he is shorter than all of his peers?
17. **Synthesis.** Taking into consideration your personal identity, what occupation do you feel you would be successful at as an adult?
18. **Synthesis.** Explain how hormones might affect your actions and emotions. Give one positive effect and one negative effect to support your answer.

Applying Health Knowledge

19. How would you explain intellectual, physical, and emotional changes in adolescence to a fifth-grade class?
20. For the next few months, keep a journal on changes you notice in your intellectual development. Make note of new abstract thinking abilities you develop as well as more complicated problems you find solutions to. Include situations when you exhibit more flexible thinking.

Beyond the Classroom

21. **Further Study.** Find a book about adolescence at your local library. Choose five definitions from this chapter to locate in the library book. Write a paragraph comparing the definitions from each source.
22. **Parental Involvement.** Take a survey of five adult family members or friends to find out whether or not they enjoyed adolescence. Have each one tell you about some of their most memorable experiences.
23. **Further Study.** Look up information about the endocrine system in a resource book. Choose two endocrine glands not discussed in this chapter. Write a paragraph about each gland, listing the hormone each gland produces and the effect of the hormone on the body.

CHAPTER

3

The Reproductive Systems

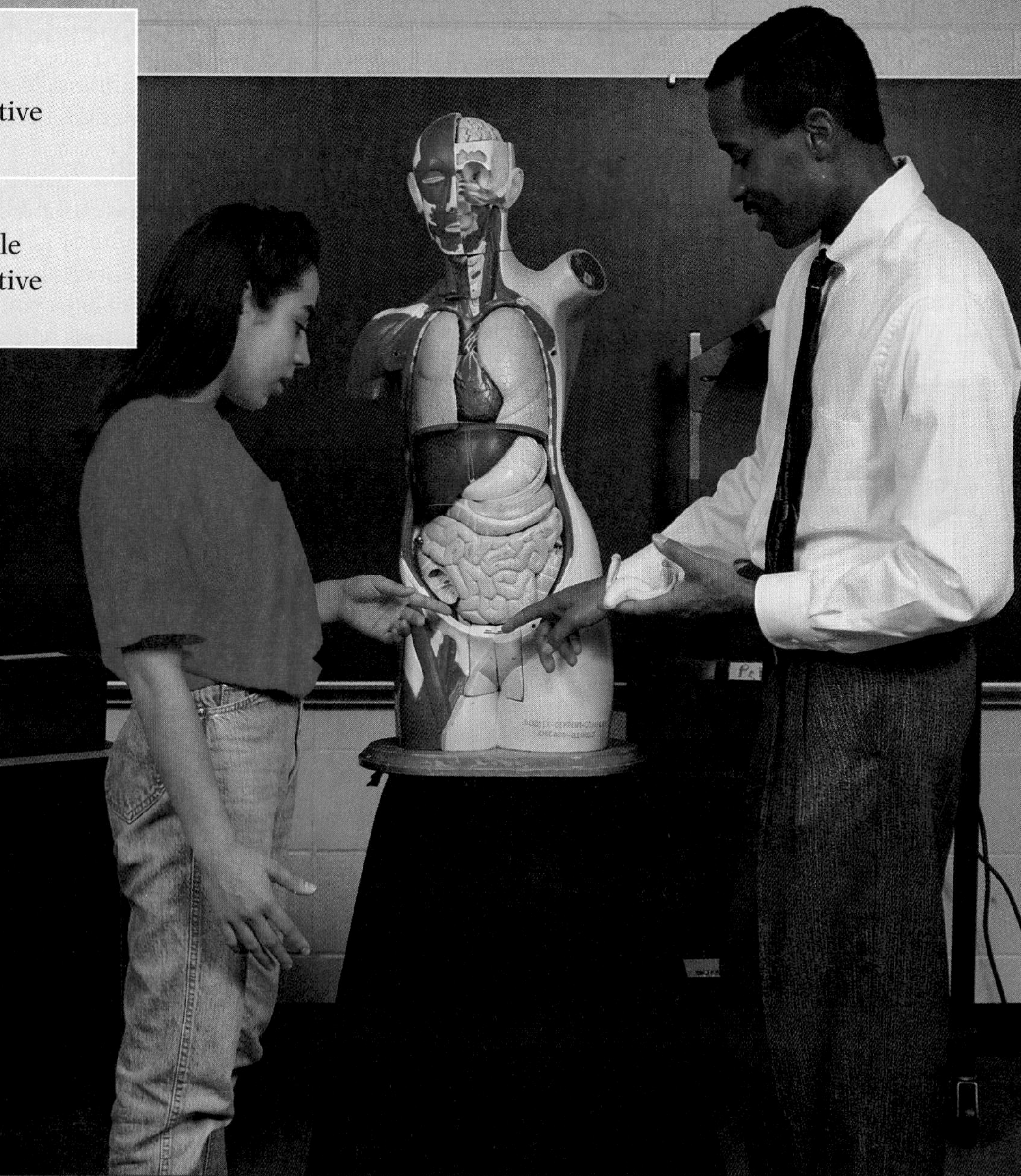

LESSON 1

THE MALE REPRODUCTIVE SYSTEM

The male reproductive system functions to produce a **sperm cell,** the male cell that unites with a female egg cell, or ovum, to form a fertilized ovum. Males do not begin producing sperm until puberty—between the ages of 12 and 15. When you studied the endocrine system, you learned that the pituitary gland secretes a hormone that causes the testes to begin producing testosterone. Testosterone causes the testes to begin producing sperm. Once a male reaches puberty and begins producing sperm, he is capable of producing sperm for the rest of his life. The process is called spermatogenesis.

LESSON 1 FOCUS

TERMS TO USE

- Sperm cell
- Testes
- Scrotum
- Epididymis (ep•uh•DID•uh•muhs)
- Penis
- Vas deferens (vas DEF•uh•ruhnz)
- Semen
- Urethra

CONCEPTS TO LEARN

- The male reproductive system functions to produce sperm.
- External male reproductive organs include the scrotum, the testes, and the penis.
- Internal male reproductive organs include the vas deferens, seminal vesicles, prostate gland, Cowper's glands, and urethra.

External Male Reproductive Organs

External male reproductive organs include the scrotum, the testes, and the penis. The **testes** are the male sex glands. They serve two important functions: they manufacture the male sex hormone, testosterone, and they produce male sex cells, called sperm. The testes hang outside the body in a sac called the **scrotum.** One testicle usually hangs slightly lower than the other.

The Scrotum

The scrotum is a loose pouch of skin that becomes darker as males grow and develop. As puberty progresses, hair will appear on the scrotum. As the testes grow, the skin of the scrotum becomes wrinkled.

The scrotum has an important function. It keeps the testes at the right temperature so they can produce sperm. The temperature of the testes must be about 3° to 4°F (1.5° to 2°C) lower than normal body temperature 98.6°F (37°C) in order to produce sperm. If body temperature rises, muscles in the scrotum relax to lower the testes away from the body. If the body temperature lowers, the muscles of the scrotum contract to pull the testes in close to the body.

The Testes

Sperm are actually produced in a section of the testes called seminiferous tubules. These are a long series of threadlike tubes packed in the testes. There are about 1,000 of these tubes, each about one to three feet long. The combined length of all the tubules can extend almost one-half mile. These tubules are capable of producing billions and billions of sperm. The testes produce 500 million or more sperm each day.

Once sperm are produced, they move into the epididymis. The **epididymis** is a highly coiled structure located on the back side of each of the testes. The epididymis stores newly produced sperm. *Epididymis* means "over the testis." The epididymis is about 20 feet in length.

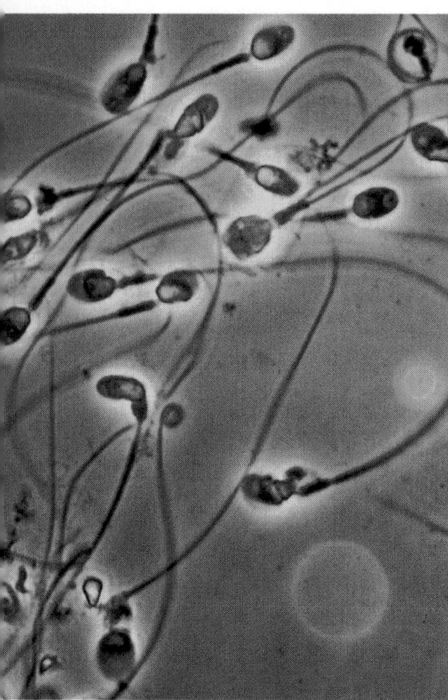

Once sperm are produced in the testes, they mature in the epididymis.

The maturation of the sperm, which began in the seminiferous tubules, continues in the epididymis. It takes about 64 days from the time sperm are produced until they become fully mature.

The Sperm Cell. A mature sperm is very tiny—about .0024 inch or 60/10,000 millimeter long. It consists of a head, a neck, a middle piece, and a tail. A normal sperm carries 23 chromosomes in the head. This is half the number of chromosomes in all the other cells of the body. When the sperm unites with an ovum, which also carries 23 chromosomes, the result is one cell of 46 chromosomes and the production of a human offspring.

The Penis

The **penis** is a tubelike organ that functions in sexual reproduction, sexual pleasure, and elimination of body wastes. The penis is normally soft and hangs downward from the front of the body at the groin area. The penis is made up of three long cylinders of spongy tissue that line up parallel to the urethra. These cylinders are tissues filled with spaces much like a sponge. They contain a very rich supply of blood vessels and nerves. When the penis is soft, these cylinders contain little blood. However, when blood from the circulatory system fills these spaces, the penis becomes hard, or erect. This process is called an erection. Contrary to what some people think, the penis is neither a muscle nor a bone. Erections result entirely from blood flow.

Erections and Ejaculation. Erections are a normal part of being a male. Boy babies have erections. However, when a male goes through puberty, hormones cause the penis to become more sensitive, and the male will have erections more often. He may have an erection at any time and for no apparent reason. This can be embarrassing, but it is perfectly normal. The penis will return to its soft state.

Penis size, both in an erect and soft state, varies. Penis size also varies from male to male. It is important to note that size has nothing to do with the male's ability to be effective in the reproductive process.

In order for semen to leave the penis, the penis must be erect. This release of semen is called ejaculation. In the small amount of semen that leaves the body—perhaps less than a teaspoonful—there are about 300 to 400 million sperm.

However, just because the penis becomes erect does not mean semen must be released. The penis can return to its soft state without an ejaculation. A male may experience some discomfort and pain if sexual arousal lasts for a period of time and he does not ejaculate. The erection goes away, but he may have a dull, sensitive, swollen feeling, especially in the testes. As the blood vessels in the penis fill with blood causing an erection, there is also a swelling of the blood vessels and muscular pressure. The testes, epididymis, vas deferens, prostate, and seminal vesicles are all involved in this reaction. They become swollen and sensitive. If pressure builds up and there is no ejaculation, it can be painful for a time. This condition is not harmful and eventually ceases.

Circumcision. All male babies are born with a fold of skin that covers the end of the penis. This is called foreskin. Circumcision is the surgical removal of the foreskin. Circumcision began as a religious custom. For many years, doctors thought it was necessary for health reasons to have a baby boy circumcised shortly after birth. Now doctors know that circumcision is not necessary for health reasons. Parents now choose whether to have their baby boy circumcised.

One difference between the circumcised and uncircumcised penis is the way the penis looks. The ridge that forms the head of the penis may be obvious on a circumcised penis. The foreskin covers this ridge on an uncircumcised penis.

It is very important for a male who is uncircumcised to wash very thoroughly every time he bathes or showers. He should pull the fold of skin back and wash under it. A substance called smegma, which is made up of dead cells and glandular secretions, can get trapped under the foreskin. Without proper health care, pathogens can grow and multiply in smegma and cause irritation and infection. Circumcised males also must wash this area.

Nocturnal Emission. As a male goes through puberty, hormones cause the glands in the reproductive system to begin producing fluids. The testes produce sperm. The seminal vesicles produce a fluid that nourishes sperm. The prostate gland produces a fluid that mixes with sperm to form semen. The fluid in the Cowper's glands cleanses the urethra.

All this new fluid causes pressure to build in the reproductive system. However, the male body has a way of relieving this pressure. At night while he is asleep, the penis becomes erect, and he will have an ejaculation. This is called a nocturnal emission. There is no warning when it occurs, and the male cannot prevent it from happening.

A nocturnal emission may or may not be accompanied by a dream. Most males experience wet dreams, or dreams dealing with sexual content, as they go through puberty. It is perfectly normal if they do experience these dreams, and it is just as normal if they do not.

The male reproductive system.

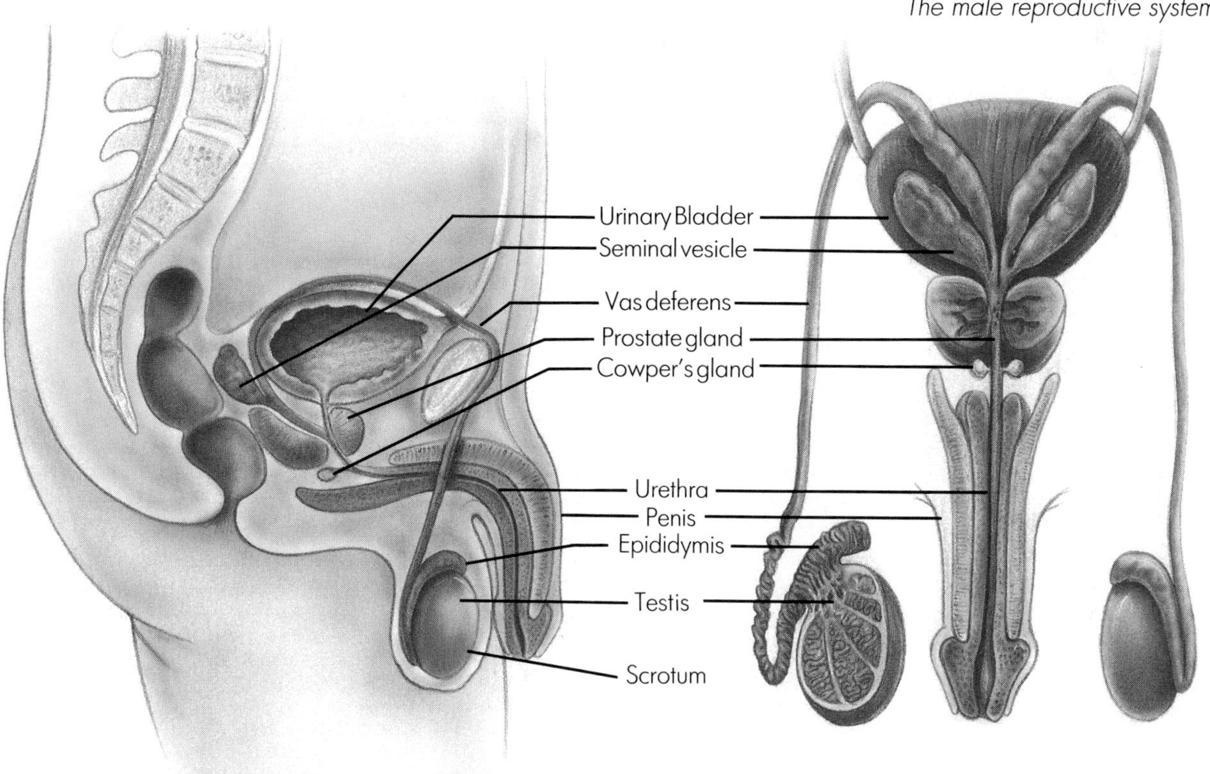

Internal Male Reproductive Organs

Internal male reproductive structures include the vas deferens, seminal vesicles, prostate gland, Cowper's glands, and urethra.

The Vas Deferens

After the sperm mature in the epididymis, they travel into another long tube, the **vas deferens,** which connects the epididymis with the urethra. There are two of these tubes, each about 18 inches long. The vas deferens are lined with cilia, fingerlike projections that help move the sperm through the tube. It is thought that while the sperm are in the epididymis and vas deferens, they have little ability to move on their own. Not until they mix with other fluids do they become mobile.

The vas deferens loops over the pubic bone, around the bladder, and through the prostate gland. As it passes through the prostate gland, it narrows and becomes the ejaculatory duct. The ejaculatory duct opens into the urethra.

The Seminal Vesicles

Look at the illustration of the male reproductive system. You will notice two little pouches just above and on either side of the prostate gland. These are the seminal vesicles (*vesicle* means "fluid-filled pouch"). The seminal vesicles secrete a fluid that mixes with the sperm. This fluid helps make the sperm mobile and provides nourishment to the sperm. The fluid from the seminal vesicles travels down the ejaculatory duct to mix with the sperm.

The Prostate Gland

The prostate gland lies just below the bladder and is about the size of a chestnut. It is made up of both muscular and glandular tissue. The prostate secretes a milky, alkaline fluid which mixes with sperm and makes up the major portion of semen. It is this solution that helps protect sperm by neutralizing the acidity of the urethra and female vagina. The mixture of sperm and fluids from the seminal vesicles, prostate gland, and Cowper's glands is called **semen.**

CANCER OF THE PROSTATE

Next to lung cancer, prostate cancer is the second highest incidence of cancer in males. The American Cancer Society projected for 1995 that there would be 244,000 cases and 40,400 deaths from this disease. Prostate cancer is most common in men 55 years of age or older. Rates are higher among blacks than whites.

Prostate cancer usually involves enlargement of the gland. However, some enlargement that is not cancerous occurs in about 50 percent of males over 50 in the United States. Any prostate enlargement can lead to a variety of urinary problems such as difficulty in urinating or controlling urination, the need to urinate frequently, painful or burning urination, or blood in the urine. Any unusual occurrence or change should be reported to a doctor.

The Cowper's Glands

Just below the prostate are two pea-sized glands that open into the urethra. These glands, the Cowper's glands, secrete a clear, sticky fluid that is thought to cleanse the urethra of acid from urine, thus allowing safe passage of sperm. The secretion causes droplets of fluid to form on the end of the penis before semen is released. These droplets of fluid can contain sperm. That means pregnancy can occur from the secretions of the Cowper's glands, even if semen never leaves the penis.

> **DID YOU KNOW?**
>
> - During fetal development, the baby boy's testes are inside his body. About two months before birth, the testes usually descend into the scrotum. In some males, only one testicle descends. The other one may not descend until years later. In some cases, a surgical procedure can correct an undescended testicle.

The Urethra

The **urethra** is a tubelike organ that travels through the penis. It leads from the ejaculatory ducts. The urethra serves as a passageway for sperm and urine. However, it is impossible for sperm and urine to leave the body at the same time. Special muscles surround the urethra at the base of the bladder. When semen is preparing to leave the body, these muscles contract to close off the bladder. Urine cannot leave through the urethra when semen is leaving the body.

Concerns About the Male Reproductive System

Hernia, sterility, and cancer of the testes are some other factors males should be aware of in promoting their health.

Hernia

A hernia is the pushing of a part of the body through the wall normally keeping it in. Hernias, therefore, may occur in various parts of the body. A common hernia of the male reproductive system is called an inguinal hernia. This is a weak spot in the abdominal wall near the top of the scrotum. Sometimes, straining the abdominal muscles can cause a tear in this spot. A part of the intestine can then push through into the scrotum. Surgery can correct this. A male can help avoid such a hernia by using care when lifting heavy objects. When lifting must be done, the male should lift with the legs rather than the back.

Sterility

Sterility in the male is a condition wherein the sperm of the male is weak, malformed, or is unable to join an ovum. Therefore, fertilization does not take place. Temperature changes, exposure to certain chemicals, smoking, contracting mumps as an adult, and faulty operation of the epididymis, vas deferens, or urethra can all result in sterility.

Each month the testes should be examined separately for changes or lumps.

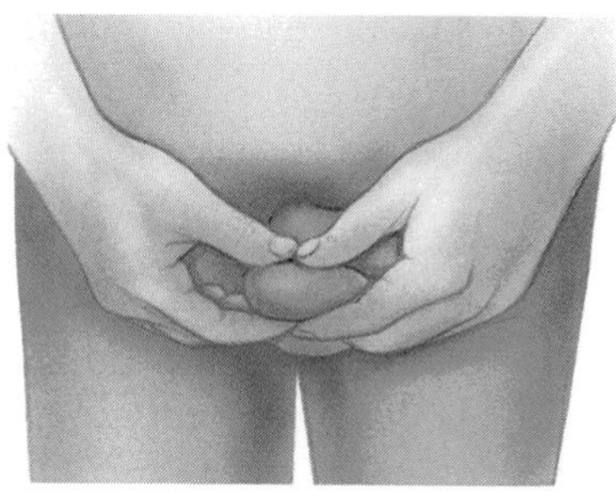

Testicular Cancer

Cancer of the testes is one of the most common cancers in men between 15 and 34 years of age. It accounts for 12 percent of all cancer deaths in this group. If discovered in the early stages, testicular cancer can be treated properly and effectively. It is important for you to take time to learn the basic facts about this type of cancer—its symptoms and treatment—and what you can do to get the help you or someone you know needs if it occurs.

The first sign of testicular cancer is usually a slight enlargement of one of the testes and a change in its consistency. There may be a small, hard lump in the testicle or a collection of fluid or blood in the scrotum. Pain may be absent, but often there is a dull ache in the lower abdomen and groin, together with a sensation of dragging and heaviness. Men who have an undescended or partially descended testicle are at a much higher risk of developing testicular cancer than others. Surgery should be done at an early age to correct this problem.

Male Reproductive Health

Care of the male reproductive system becomes important as a person goes through puberty. Cleanliness is important to prevent body odor.

Testicular Self-Examination

Early detection of testicular cancer can be accomplished with a simple three-minute monthly self-examination. The best time is after a warm bath or shower, when the scrotal skin is relaxed. The male rolls each testicle gently between the thumb and fingers of both hands. If there are any hard lumps or nodules on a testicle, he should see his doctor promptly. The testicle may not be cancerous, but only a doctor can make such a diagnosis. Following a thorough physical examination, the doctor may perform certain tests to make the most accurate diagnosis possible. Self-examination for testicular cancer should be done by all males from puberty to 50 years of age.

LESSON 1 REVIEW

Reviewing Facts and Vocabulary

1. Name one male reproductive disorder and define it.
2. Name two ways to care for the male reproductive system.
3. What is the main function of the male reproductive system?
4. List the external and internal male reproductive organs.

Thinking Critically

5. **Evaluation.** How would you respond if your best friend told you he was worried because he had an ejaculation in his sleep?
6. **Synthesis.** How might the male reproductive system be affected if the vas deferens did not function properly?

Applying Health Knowledge

7. Choose one disorder of the male reproductive system not mentioned in this lesson. Research it further and prepare a written report that defines the disorder and suggests ways to prevent and treat it.

LESSON 2

THE FEMALE REPRODUCTIVE SYSTEM

The reproductive system is the only system in the body that has different organs for the male and female. The female reproductive system functions to produce an ovum, which, when united with a sperm cell, forms a fertilized ovum.

LESSON 2 FOCUS

TERMS TO USE

- Vulva
- Vagina
- Cervix
- Uterus
- Fallopian (fuh•LOH•pee•uhn) tubes
- Ovaries
- Ovulation
- Menstruation

CONCEPTS TO LEARN

- The female reproductive system functions to produce ova.
- External female reproductive organs are the vulva, which includes the clitoris, mons pubis, labia majora, labia minora, and vaginal opening.
- The internal female reproductive organs include the vagina, uterus, Fallopian tubes, and ovaries.

Female External Reproductive Organs

The organs of the female reproductive system are primarily internal. The external organs are called the **vulva.** They consist of the clitoris, mons pubis, labia majora (outer lips), labia minora (inner lips), and the vaginal opening.

The Clitoris

The clitoris is a small knob of tissue in front of the vaginal opening. It has a rich supply of nerve endings and blood vessels. The clitoris has no known reproductive function. It does, however, have an important function in producing sexual arousal.

The Mons Pubis and Labia

The mons pubis is a rounded fatty pad of tissue, covered with pubic hair. It is located in the front of the female body. The mons pubis is directly on top of the pubic bone.

The labia majora is the outer fold of tissue on either side of the vaginal opening. These outer folds are also covered with pubic hair. The inner folds of skin are called labia minora. They are just inside the labia majora. These inner folds extend forward forming a hoodlike covering over the clitoris. Both the inner and outer labia are rich in nerve endings and blood vessels. The labia serve as a line of protection against pathogens entering the body and also serve a function in sexual arousal.

The Vaginal Opening

The vaginal opening becomes visible when the labia are parted. Just inside the vaginal opening may be a thin membrane called the hymen. This membrane stretches across the opening of the vagina. It has no known function and is not present in all females. The hymen usually has several openings in it, thus allowing for the passage of the menstrual flow.

Throughout history, there have been many misconceptions about the hymen. It was thought that an intact hymen was the sign of a virgin—a person who has not had sexual intercourse. It was also thought that with first intercourse and the tearing of the hymen, a female experienced pain and bleeding. Neither of these beliefs are true. Some females are born without a hymen. Others may tear the hymen through a variety of physical activities—often without even knowing it.

Some hymen tissue is very flexible and may stay intact during intercourse. Because there are usually openings in the hymen, sperm released at the vaginal opening can swim into the vagina and up to an ovum, resulting in fertilization and pregnancy. Thus, a female could become pregnant and still have an intact hymen.

Female Internal Reproductive Organs

The internal organs of the female reproductive system are the vagina, uterus, Fallopian tubes, and ovaries.

The Vagina

The **vagina** is a very elastic, tubelike passageway, about four to five inches long. Also called the birth canal, the vagina is capable of stretching to allow for the birth of a baby. In its resting state, the walls of the vagina touch each other. During sexual arousal, these walls expand to allow for entrance of the penis.

The vagina leads to the **cervix,** or neck of the uterus. The cervical opening is very small. During childbirth, the cervix dilates, or opens, to allow passage of the baby.

The female reproductive system.

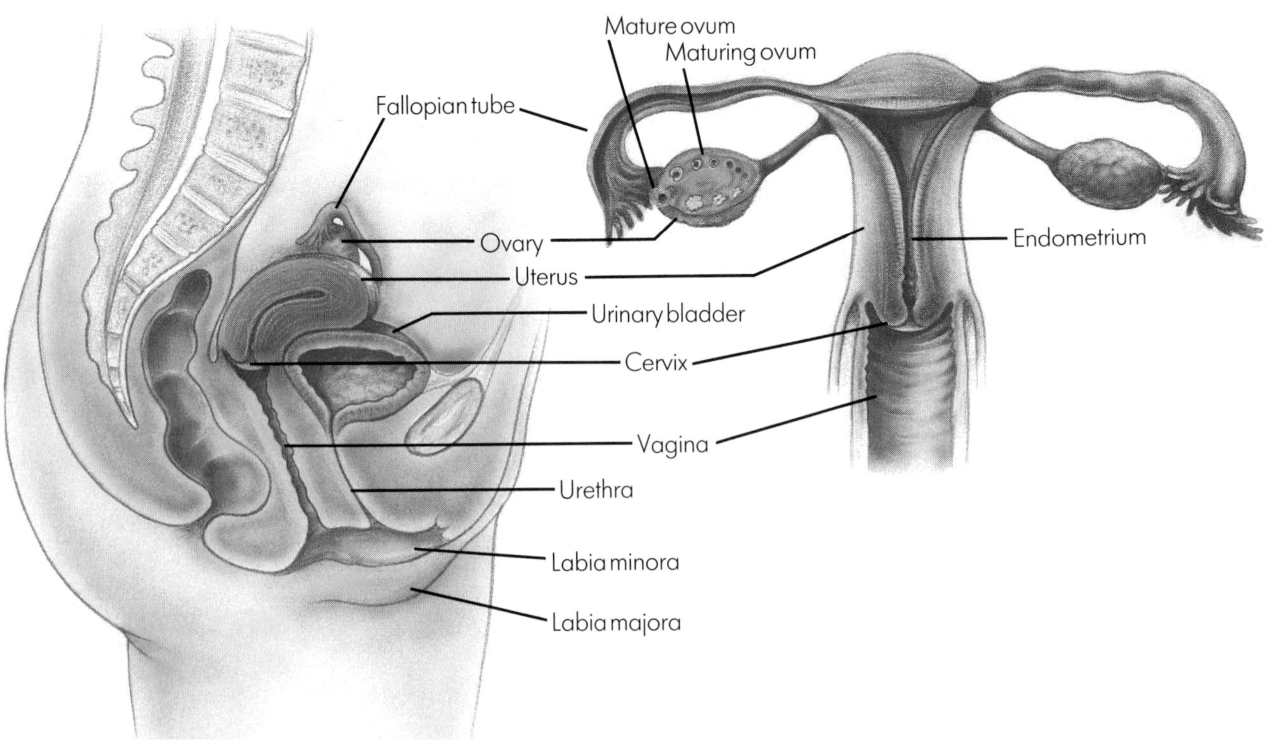

The Uterus

The **uterus** is a very strong, elastic muscle, about the size of a fist. The primary function of the uterus is to hold and nourish the developing embryo and fetus. The uterus has an inner lining called endometrium, which is richly supplied with blood vessels. It is this lining that builds up with blood tissue each month to prepare for a possible pregnancy.

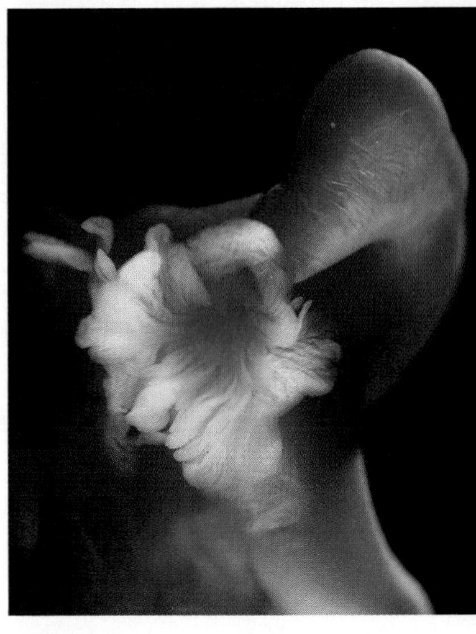

Ovulation occurs when an ovary releases an ovum into the ovary's Fallopian tube. The ovum would enter the Fallopian tube, as shown here.

The Fallopian Tubes

On each side of the uterus are tubes called **Fallopian tubes.** The Fallopian tubes are extremely narrow and are lined with hairlike projections called cilia. Fimbriae, fingerlike projections at the end of the Fallopian tubes, surround the top part of the ovaries. The cilia in the fimbria gather a released ovum into the Fallopian tube. Fertilization of the ovum usually occurs in the widest part of the Fallopian tube.

The Ovaries

The **ovaries** are the female sex glands situated on both sides of the uterus. They have two important functions. They house the ova and produce the female sex hormones estrogen and progesterone.

Ovulation. At birth, a female usually has about 200,000 to 300,000 immature ova in her ovaries. As she enters puberty, hormones from the pituitary gland cause the ovaries to begin producing the female sex hormones. The ova begin to mature. Each month, one ovary releases one mature ovum into that ovary's Fallopian tube. This is called **ovulation.** The ovum can live about two days in the Fallopian tube. If at any time during this period sperm are present, one sperm will enter the ovum. This is called fertilization, or conception. Pregnancy begins at that point.

Preparation of the Uterus. Each month, the uterus begins to prepare for a possible pregnancy by building up a rich, thick layer of blood and other tissue. Hormones produced in the ovaries cause this thickening of the uterine lining. If the ovum is fertilized, it moves into the uterus and attaches to this lining. It is here the ovum will divide millions of times over the nine months of pregnancy and develop into a human being.

Menstruation. If the ovum is not fertilized, it dies and passes into the uterus. Then the uterine lining is not needed because there is no pregnancy. The muscles of the uterus contract, causing the lining to gradually break down. This lining passes through the vagina and out of the body. This procedure is called **menstruation.** The menstrual period usually lasts 4 to 7 days, but in some females it may last 3 days and in others 9 or 10 days. The menstrual period is regulated by hormones and will vary from female to female.

A female loses about two to three tablespoons of blood during the menstrual period. The rest of the menstrual flow is other tissue that makes up the lining of the uterus. This is blood and tissue that the body does not need, therefore the menstrual period does not make a person weak or ill.

DID YOU KNOW?

- Cervical cancer is one of the most common types of cancer in females.
- The earlier a female begins to have sexual intercourse, the greater her chances are of developing cervical cancer. The more sexual partners she has, the more a female's risk is increased.
- Cervical cancer can be detected by a Pap smear. Early detection is important in successfully treating this cancer.

MYTHS ABOUT MENSTRUATION

There are many myths about menstruation. Years ago, before we knew how the female reproductive system worked, people found various ways to explain the cycle. It is not hard to see why there were so many wrong ideas. However, today we know how and why menstruation occurs, so we can dispel these wrong ideas. Some common myths include:

- A female should not bathe or shower during her period. (Cleanliness is essential, especially during this time. Once a female reaches puberty, she should bathe or shower daily.)
- A female should not wash her hair during her period.
- A female should not have a tooth cavity filled during her period.
- A female should not swim or participate in physical activity during her period.

All of these are false. A female can carry on her normal activities during menstruation. One additional misconception is that a female cannot get pregnant if she has intercourse during her menstrual period. This is not true. A female can get pregnant during her period. Sperm can live for five to seven days in the female body and may overlap the period between the end of one menstrual cycle and the beginning of another ovulation. Remember, it is very unlikely that a teen would know when an ovum is in a Fallopian tube. If an ovum has been released and if sperm are present, fertilization can occur.

After the period ends, the menstrual cycle begins again. An ovum matures and is released from an ovary. The lining of the uterus begins to build up blood and tissue again. If the ovum is fertilized, it attaches to the lining. If it is not fertilized, the lining breaks down and there is another menstrual period.

Because the uterus contracts to break down the lining, the female may experience abdominal cramps at the beginning of the menstrual period. Menstrual cramps are usually mild, lasting several hours. Light exercise can help relieve cramps. A warm bath or a heating pad might also help to relax muscles. However, severe or persistent cramping may be an indication that medical attention is necessary.

The menstrual period occurs when an ovum is not fertilized and the lining of the uterus breaks down.

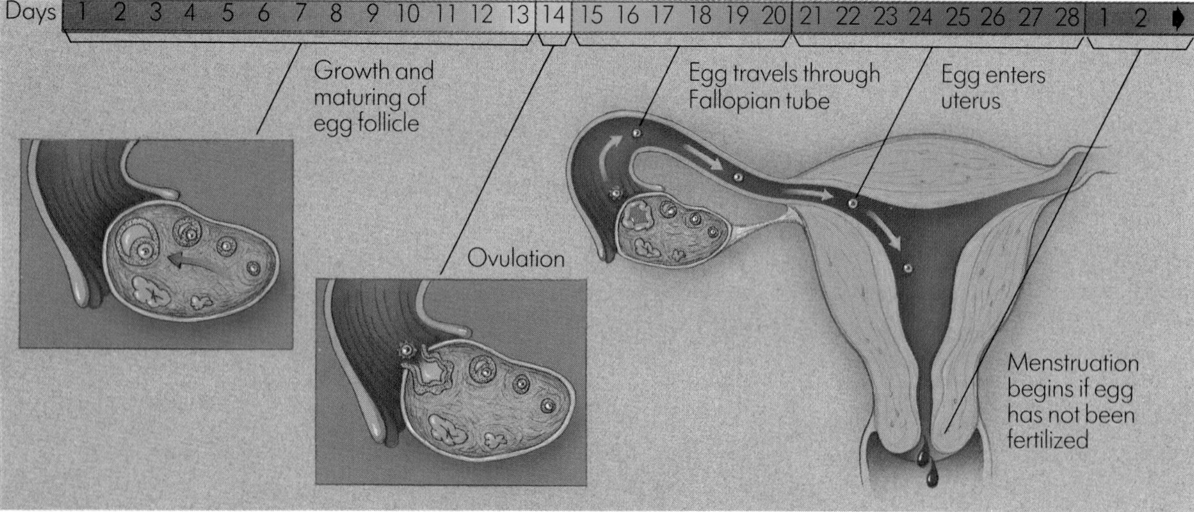

Almost all females begin menstruating between the ages of 10 and 15. It takes the body a couple of years to adjust to all of the changes it is experiencing at this time. For this reason, the menstrual cycle is likely to be irregular during this time.

Hormones control the menstrual cycle. However, nutrition, stress, and illness also can also influence the cycle.

Menstrual Health Care. Health care is important all the time, but it is especially important during the menstrual period. There should not be an odor from the vagina at any time. There is no odor to the menstrual flow until it mixes with air. A female should take a bath or shower every day, washing and rinsing thoroughly.

If a female uses sanitary napkins or panty shields to catch the menstrual flow, she should change them every three to four hours, depending on how heavy her menstrual flow is. Some people use tampons to catch the menstrual flow. These are cylinders of a cotton material and are placed inside the vagina. They must be changed frequently and should not be worn at night. Tampons left in for more than a four-hour period increase a person's risk of infection.

DID YOU KNOW?

- Toxic shock syndrome (TSS) is a rare disease caused by infection with varieties of the common bacterium *Staphylococcus aureus*. More than half of all cases occur in women, but TSS has also been diagnosed in men and children.
- Symptoms of TSS include a high fever, vomiting, diarrhea, low blood pressure, dizziness, fainting, and a rash resembling sunburn.
- Among women, TSS has been traced to use of super-absorbent tampons that absorb magnesium, enabling toxins to flourish. Preventive measures include avoidance or intermittent use of tampons.
- TSS can be treated with antibiotics, fluids, and other supportive therapy. For the most part TSS is curable, however in 5 percent of cases, it is fatal.

Concerns About the Female Reproductive System

As with any body system, there can be problems with the female reproductive system. It is important for a female to be familiar with her body and know when common problems might occur.

Sterility

Sterility in the female takes a number of forms. One cause of female sterility is a blocking of one or both Fallopian tubes. When this happens, ova cannot pass into the uterus. Another cause of sterility occurs when the female does not ovulate. A third cause of female sterility is endometriosis, a condition in which endometrial tissue grows outside the uterus in other areas of the pelvic cavity. Surgery can sometimes correct this condition.

Premenstrual Syndrome (PMS)

Premenstrual syndrome (PMS) refers to a variety of symptoms that some females experience before their menstrual periods. Symptoms vary and may be experienced two weeks to several days before the menstrual period. Many females never experience PMS.

The symptoms of PMS include nervous tension, anxiety, irritability, bloating, weight gain, depression, mood swings, and fatigue. The causes of PMS are not completely understood, but it seems to be more common in women in their 30s. Some doctors believe that PMS is related to a hormonal imbalance. Others attribute the cause to a nutritional deficiency.

Most doctors recommend diet and life-style changes as the first treatment of PMS. They also encourage women to find ways to reduce stress.

Perform monthly breast self-exam:

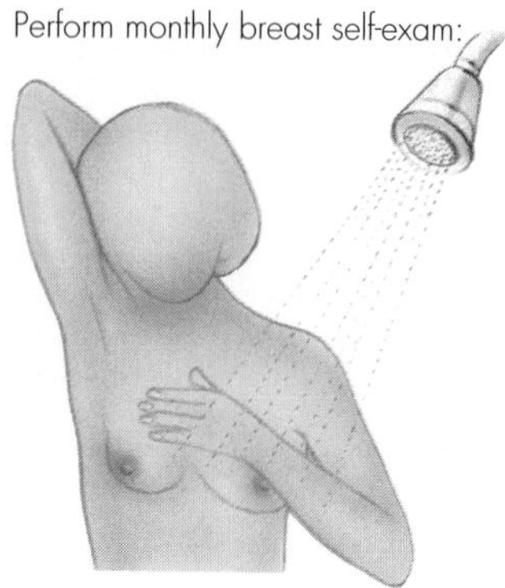

(A) in the shower or during a bath—feel for a lump or thickening with the hand opposite to the breast;

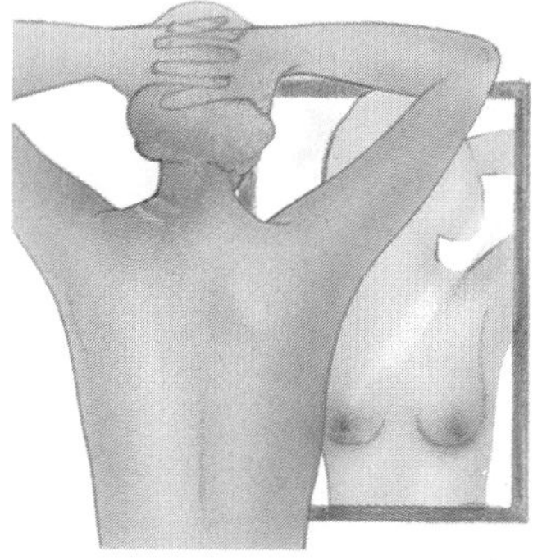

(B) before a mirror—inspect the breasts with arms at the sides then with arms raised; look for changes in the size and shape of each breast, look for dimpling, check again with palms at hips while flexing chest muscles;

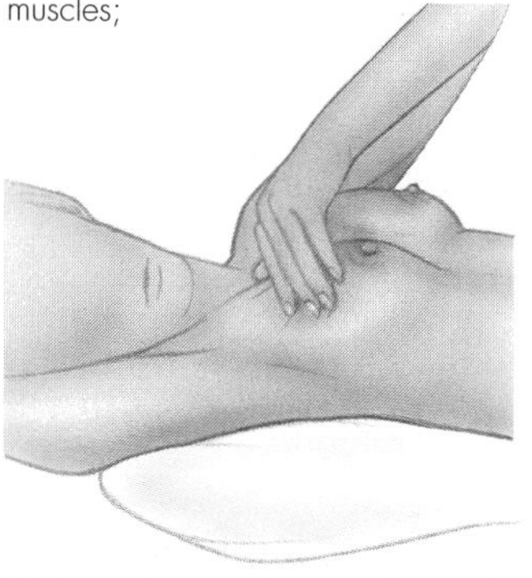

(C) lying down—place a pillow or folded towel under your shoulder and examine the breast;

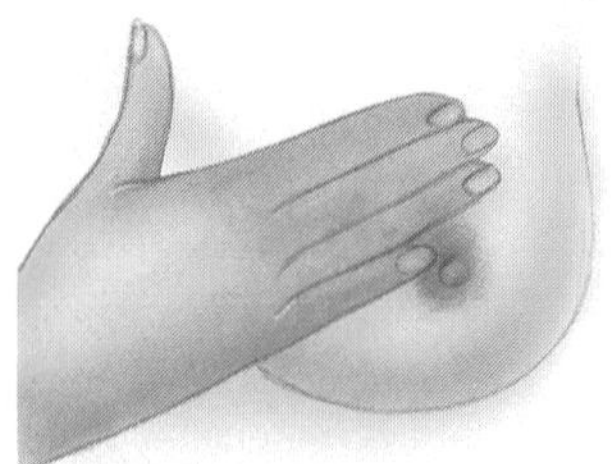

(D) with fingers flat, begin at the outermost edge of the breast and press in small circles spiraling in toward the nipple; squeeze the nipple and look for any discharge.

PMS sufferers should reduce their intake of sugar, salt, caffeine, nicotine, and alcoholic beverages. They should also increase their intake of B vitamins, magnesium, leafy green vegetables, whole grains, and fruit. Finally, a regular exercise program should be followed.

Dysmenorrhea

Dysmenorrhea consists of painful contractions in the uterus during menstruation. A warm bath or doing exercises can usually bring relief. If pain continues, a doctor should be consulted.

Vaginitis

Vaginitis refers to vaginal infections and is a very common condition in females. It will affect most females at some point during their lives. There are several types of vaginal infections. The three most common are yeast infection, nonspecific vaginitis, and trichomoniasis.

- Yeast Infection. The signs of yeast infection, which is caused by a fungus, are a thick, white discharge and genital itching.
- Nonspecific Vaginitis. This infection is caused by bacteria. Symptoms include itching, an odorless discharge, and a burning sensation during urination.
- Trichomoniasis. This infection often occurs at the end of the menstrual period and is caused by a protozoan, a small living organism. The symptoms include an odorous discharge, genital itching, and occasionally a burning sensation during urination.

Breast Cancer

Breast cancer is the second leading cause of death in women after lung cancer. The American Cancer Society projected in 1995 that there would be 182,000 cases during the year with 46,240 deaths. Male breast cancer would account for 240 of those deaths. Two-thirds of cases occur in women more than 50 years old, but breast cancer does occur in younger women as well.

No one knows exactly what causes breast cancer, so there is little anyone can do to prevent it. However, it is known that breast cancer is most treatable and curable when the tumor is small. Also, treatment may be more limited and less disfiguring if the cancer is found when it is confined to a small area of the breast. For these reasons cancer research scientists have long looked for methods of detecting or finding breast cancer early in its growth, before it has had a chance to spread to other parts of the body. Studies show that females with a family history of breast cancer develop the disease at about twice the average rate.

Symptoms of breast cancer for both males and females include:

- change in breast or nipple appearance
- lump or swelling in the breast
- lump under the armpit

Ninety percent of all breast lumps in females are discovered by the females themselves—most of the lumps are benign, or harmless.

HEALTH UPDATE

LOOKING AT TECHNOLOGY

Breast Cancer: Prevention and Treatment

Years ago a diagnosis of cancer meant a person had almost no hope of survival. Today the cure rate, or no sign of cancer 5 years after treatment, is close to 50 percent. There were about 182,000 cases of breast cancer in 1995. About 11 percent of all females will get it. Breast cancer does not often occur before age 25. The average age of diagnosis is at age 52. Females at increased risk are those with a family history of breast cancer.

Breast self-examination done a week or two after the menstrual cycle helps detect possible bumps or dimpling of the breasts or changes in the nipple.

Another method of early detection is mammography, when the breast is pressed between two plates and an X ray of the breast is taken. Mammography is advised for females beginning at age 35 to 40. The amount of radiation received during mammography is small. Mammography can reveal signs of cancer up to two years before symptoms appear.

If breast cancer is detected, several treatment options are available. These include surgery, radiotherapy, hormonal treatment, chemotherapy, and adjuvant therapy.

- Surgery—radical mastectomy involves surgical removal of the mammary nodes including underlying muscle.
- Surgery—modified mastectomy involves removal of the cancerous part of the breast or tumor on the breast. This is also called a lumpectomy.
- Radiotherapy—radiation is used to remove tumors and axillary nodes. It is often used with a form of surgery, such as a lumpectomy.
- Hormonal treatment—some hormonal suppression and control can be used to treat cancer that has dispersed to other parts of the body.
- Chemotherapy—chemicals are used that affect dividing cancerous cells more than normal tissues.
- Adjuvant therapy—the use of hormones or medicines after surgery to destroy any remaining cancer cells so no new growth can begin.

Female Reproductive Health

Just as it is important to develop good health habits to promote one's overall health, females also can choose behaviors that affect reproductive health.

The Breast Self-Examination

Doing a breast self-exam (BSE) is an important health habit. The best time to perform a BSE is about one week after your menstrual period. It is also important to have regular mammograms beginning at age 35.

The Pelvic Examination

The American Cancer Society recommends that as soon as a female begins to have sexual intercourse, or when she turns 18, she should begin having a yearly pelvic examination. The pelvic examination is extremely important in the detection of cervical cancer. Early detection is the key to a cure.

Some females may feel embarrassed or fearful about having a pelvic examination. A female should talk with her doctor to know ahead of time everything that will be done during the exam. If the female knows what to expect and is relaxed, the exam should not be painful.

The health professional will ask the female questions about her health history. The female also should ask any questions or share any concerns that she has about her health. A general exam may be done to check blood pressure, the heart, and the lungs. Urine and blood tests are usually done. The female's breasts and abdomen are checked for lumps.

The doctor then checks the external genital area to be sure that everything looks normal. Next, the doctor will do a digital exam of the vagina and other tissue. Then, to help the doctor see inside, a speculum is used to hold the walls of the vagina open. This instrument may be metal or plastic and comes in different sizes. When the doctor is careful and the patient is relaxed, insertion of the speculum should not be painful. However, there are some very strong muscles in the pelvic area. If the female is tense, the patient might experience some discomfort.

Once the speculum is in place, the doctor can perform a Pap smear by taking cells from the cervix. A long instrument, similar to a cotton swab, is used to gather the cells and place them on a slide for laboratory examination. It is from these cells that cancer or a precancerous condition is detected.

LESSON 2 REVIEW

Reviewing Facts and Vocabulary

1. List the external and internal female reproductive organs.
2. What are two functions of the ovaries?
3. What part of the female sexual anatomy has no known reproductive function?

Thinking Critically

4. **Synthesis.** Explain what might occur if a fertilized ovum became implanted in a Fallopian tube.
5. **Synthesis.** How might you respond if a friend told you she always experiences PMS the week after her menstrual period?

Applying Health Knowledge

6. A mature ovum has just been released from an ovary. Write a short story about the ovum's experiences for the next few weeks. Indicate whether or not the ovum becomes fertilized and what will occur after that point.

CHAPTER 3

REVIEW

Reviewing Facts and Vocabulary

1. Define *spermatogenesis* and discuss what leads to this process.
2. Explain the function of the scrotum.
3. Some people think erections are due to muscle or bone in the penis becoming hard. Explain whether this is true or not.
4. Discuss the functions of the uterus.
5. Name three symptoms of breast cancer.
6. What action may result in an inguinal hernia?
7. What is the tubelike organ that travels through the penis?
8. Name three causes of sterility in males.
9. How much blood does a female normally lose during her menstrual period?
10. Should females use tampons during the night when they are asleep?
11. At what age do most females begin menstruating?
12. Define *endometriosis.*

Thinking Critically

13. **Synthesis.** What would you say to someone who told you it is okay to have sex while a female is menstruating because she cannot get pregnant?
14. **Evaluation.** What are some good health decisions you can make to care for your reproductive system?
15. **Synthesis.** Explain why a female may become pregnant if the penis never enters her vagina and the male ejaculates outside her vagina.
16. **Synthesis.** In the reproductive process, how many chromosomes are needed to produce a healthy offspring? Explain your answer in a paragraph.
17. **Synthesis.** What is unique about the male and female reproductive systems when compared to the other systems of the body?
18. **Analysis.** What is the relationship between ovulation, fertilization, and menstruation?

Applying Health Knowledge

19. Sometimes a fertilized ovum fails to move through the Fallopian tube to the uterus. Instead, the zygote continues to grow in the Fallopian tube. Why would it be impossible for this to be a normal pregnancy? What problems may occur?
20. Your friend has told you in confidence that she has had an unusual vaginal discharge for several days. She is worried but afraid to tell anyone else. What would you do to help her?
21. Your 11-year-old brother asks you what a "wet dream" is. What would you tell him?

Beyond the Classroom

22. **Further Study.** At the library, research the pregnancy and birthing process. Interview one female who has experienced pregnancy and birth. Present your research to the class.
23. **Parental Involvement.** Invite parents to the classroom to discuss issues that teenagers are often faced with concerning puberty and reproductive health. List positive ways that teenagers can promote their reproductive health.
24. **Parental Involvement.** Discuss with your parents numerous feminine health care ads that are shown on television and found in magazines. Discuss ways to determine whether or not a particular product is a good one to use.
25. **Further Study.** Choose a disease related to the male or female reproductive system. Do research to find the cause, effects, and treatment of this disease. Write a two-page paper that also includes measures that can be taken to prevent this disease.
26. **Community Involvement.** Contact the American Cancer Society to get information about cancer and the reproductive system. Report your findings to the class.

CHAPTER

4 Relationships and Decisions About Sex

OUR RELATIONSHIPS

We are born as social beings. That means we need other people. People enrich our lives. You have learned that a basic emotional need we all have is the need to belong. We need to feel that we are valued members of a group. Throughout our lives, we will become members of many groups of people.

LESSON 1 FOCUS

TERMS TO USE

- Value
- Communication
- Conflict

CONCEPTS TO LEARN

- Your relationships help satisfy a basic emotional need to belong.
- You must identify and express your expectations for relationships to be healthy.
- You can learn from conflict in your relationships.

Family Relationships

The first group most people belong to is their family. Our first experiences with other people are usually with our family. There, we learn how to get along with others. Our basic value system comes from our family. A **value** is a principle that is important to you. You apply values to decisions you must make.

The family, as the basic unit of society, serves two essential functions:

- First, it is the primary support system to which individuals turn in order to have their basic needs met.
- Second, it provides the essential mechanism by which a child, born with nothing but potential, develops the capability to survive and function in this world.

From the family comes the first opportunities for physical well-being, learning, and loving. Some psychologists believe that a child's intelligence and personality are almost developed by age four or five. The child's primary environment during those early years is usually in the family.

Relationships With Friends

As we grow, our environment expands. We begin to have experiences and meet people outside of home and family. We make new and different friends. We learn more about ourselves and others as we develop these relationships. Think of friends that you had as a child. What factors made those people friends? What activities did you do together?

As we get older, some of the types of friendships we have change. They mature as we do. You may still have many of the same friendships that you had in childhood. Think of how those relationships have changed and grown. It is usually when relationships do not grow that they eventually end.

Relationships in Adolescent Years

Remember the basic tasks of adolescence discussed in Chapter 2. One very important task involves forming more mature relationships with peers of both sexes. Many of the activities—especially school activities—during the teen years support working on this developmental task.

Being involved in a variety of school, church, and community activities helps a young person grow socially. It also helps build a person's confidence in social settings.

Dating

Dating is an important social activity for many adolescents. Many times group dates offer opportunities to meet and interact with a variety of people. These types of social situations also reduce some of the pressure of asking someone out or being asked out. During group dates, you can get to know someone a little better in a more informal setting. This makes the transition to going out on a date as a couple a little easier. Some of the typical nervousness and awkwardness of first dates can be lessened with group social interaction.You may decide, however, that the person is someone you do not want to go out with in the future. That is fine. It does not mean there is anything wrong with the other person. It means that you do not think the person is someone with whom you want to form a dating relationship.

It is easy to get your feelings of self-worth wrapped up into whether someone else likes you. If there is rejection or if a relationship breaks up, you may think, "I am not good enough," or "Something is wrong with me." This is absolutely not true. It really means that the other person has different preferences or interests than you and chooses not to go out with you. Rejection is difficult, and breaking up, especially if it was an important relationship, is painful. However, it is important not to lose your feelings of self-worth because of another person.

Remember adolescence is a time to meet and date a variety of people. As you do, you learn more about yourself. You learn traits and characteristics in others that you like and do not like. All this knowledge can help you choose a partner if you decide to marry.

Going Together. Dating often leads to going together. There are some advantages to doing so. However, teenagers who go together and who have dated very little may be closing themselves off too early in their social development from meeting other people. Going together is convenient and ensures you of having a date, but it may not be helpful in developing other healthy relationships. Steady dating also may lead to sexual involvement.

Stages of grief can be experienced with the loss of a relationship.

BROKEN RELATIONSHIPS

Anytime we suffer a significant loss, we experience grief. The intensity of the grief depends on the loss—the end of a meaningful relationship, the breakup of one's family, the death of a pet, or the death of a family member.

A noted psychiatrist, Elisabeth Kübler-Ross, has identified stages people who were dying experience. She studied the process they went through until they accepted death. She, along with others who work in this field, now believe that people go through similar stages with any significant loss.

Stage 1: Denial and Isolation. Denial is a person's initial reaction to a significant loss. It may be a feeling of isolation or helplessness. It is an attempt to avoid reality by saying or thinking, "It is all a bad dream and will go away."

Stage 2: Anger. A person moves from denial to the second stage—anger. Anger is a natural reaction, an outlet for resentment at being a victim. There may be envy of others who have not experienced such a loss. The person often takes out the anger on those close by—friends and family.

Stage 3: Bargaining. Anger is often followed by a bargaining stage. The person seeks to postpone the loss by making promises, often to God, to be a better person. "I'll do this, if you will only do. . . ."

Stage 4: Depression. The fourth stage, depression, follows feelings of isolation and loneliness. The numbness, anger, and rage felt previously are now replaced with a sense of great loss. Depression causes feelings of helplessness.

Stage 5: Acceptance. The fifth stage is that of acceptance. Acceptance involves facing reality in a constructive way. It allows for action.

One of the most significant losses a young person may experience is the breakup of a relationship. If the person was in love for the first time and had invested a great deal of personal involvement in the relationship, the loss is intensified. Understanding the normal stages of grief may help you better cope with a significant loss.

Communication

Whatever the reasons for dating and going together, if the relationship is to be healthy, you must identify and express your expectations—the rules or guidelines by which you are operating. By doing this, you open the doors to **communication**—exchange of information between or among people. Your date can respond or react and also share his or her expectations. This open type of discussion is not easy. It takes practice, but it can be very helpful in preventing misunderstandings. The verbal or nonverbal expression of feelings, thoughts, and ideas is crucial to any relationship.

Good Communication Skills

Good communication means clearly stating what you are feeling and what you want. Here are some suggestions. Practice them when there is not a problem—then you will be more likely to use them when faced with a problem.

1. Start all of your statements with the word *I*.
2. Tell what happened and how you feel.

DID YOU KNOW?

- During communication, what is said can be mixed up at any of the following eight points. There is what you intended to say, what you actually say, what the other person hears, what that person says to him- or herself about what he or she heard, what that person intends to say back, what is actually said back to you, what you hear, and what you say to yourself about what you heard.
- Practicing speaking and listening skills can help promote better communication.

Good communication includes listening to others.

3. Try not to use the word *you.* By using the word *I,* you are taking responsibility for how you feel rather than blaming someone else. Usually when people are blamed or accused of something, they try to defend themselves. When you use *I,* other people have no need to be defensive and are more likely to talk about the problem.
4. Tell the other person how your concern involves him or her.
5. Tell what you would like to have happen. Try to avoid using *you.*

Following these steps does not ensure that you will solve the problem. The other person may choose not to talk about the problem. You have no control over how the other person responds or reacts. However, you have expressed your feelings in a healthy, constructive manner, and you will feel better for doing it.

Good Listening Skills

Have you ever noticed that good listeners are often well-liked people? Everyone wants to feel that he or she is being heard and is not going to be judged, corrected, or interrupted. People like a good listener. Good communication means clearly stating what you are feeling or what you want. It also means really listening to what the other person is saying. Follow these guidelines for being a good listener:

- Give your full attention to the person speaking. Eliminate distractions. If a loud radio or television is distracting you from hearing what someone is saying, turn it off.
- Focus on the speaker's message by looking for the central concept. Try to get the point of what someone is saying rather than trying to remember every fact the speaker mentions.
- Indicate your interest. Lean toward the speaker; nod at or encourage the other person by saying "Uh-huh" or "I see," in a quiet voice. Make eye contact.
- Remember what the speaker has said and, to be sure you heard it correctly, repeat the point so the person can correct you, if necessary. When it's your turn to speak, recap the highlights of what the other person has said, using a phrase like, "As I understood it, you were saying. . . ."

Conflict

Conflict is strong disagreement or opposition between persons. Conflict can happen in any relationship. Conflicts occur in relationships for many different reasons. Some of the most common reasons include lack of communication between two people, or the attempt to meet different strong needs. Sometimes one person brings a specific purpose to the conflict—perhaps to win or to dominate. Conflict occurs when one person is defending, while the other is attacking or thought to be attacking.

Sometimes a conflict results when one person already has an impression of what the other person is like. The person bases his or her impression on some previous experience, making a judgment about the other person that may or may not be accurate.

There are times when individuals themselves are not confident, and they perceive any topic that is brought up as a threat to them. Thus, they become very anxious, and this situation can cause conflict, too.

Positive Aspects of Conflict

Conflict is not all bad. It can have some constructive results, depending on how a person handles it. Here are some ways that conflict can be constructive:

- Conflicts can make people more aware of problems that they need to resolve.
- Conflicts can help individuals begin to know themselves better and to know what annoys them.
- Conflicts encourage change, keeping individuals from maintaining old habits when they need to review and change.
- Conflicts can usually reduce the small irritations in relationships. They can serve to clear the air.
- Conflicts can make life more interesting by causing a person to look more deeply into an issue, particularly from a new perspective.
- Conflicts can help to deepen and improve a relationship, strengthening each person's belief that the bond between the individuals is stronger than any issue causing conflict.

Conflict and Dating

Both people on a date must be willing to express themselves and to listen to what the other person is saying. Dating provides you an opportunity to practice your communication skills and work through conflicts.

Suppose you are on a date with someone you really like. You've gotten to know each other, and you have fun together. What are some expectations you might have of the person you are dating? Are male and female expectations different? How would your date know what your expectations are?

Conflict can occur when two people's expectations are different and are not clearly communicated. Good communication is a major key to a good relationship.

LESSON 1 REVIEW

Reviewing Facts and Vocabulary

1. Name the two essential functions of the family.
2. Define *value* and tell why values are important.
3. List two benefits of group dating.
4. Name two good communication skills and two good listening skills.

Thinking Critically

5. **Synthesis.** Give an example in which conflict might help a relationship.
6. **Synthesis.** Name at least four good communication or listening skills that you would use in a job interview.
7. **Evaluation.** What would you think of a close friend who became angry and mean to you after her boyfriend ended their relationship and you had nothing to do with it?

Applying Health Knowledge

8. Make a list of positive ways you can develop healthy relationships with your peers. Name some things you can do to become a good friend.

Decisions About Sexual Relationships and Sexual Violence

LESSON 2 FOCUS

Terms to Use

- Sexual response cycle
- Rape
- Incest

Concepts to Learn

- Communication is critical in the area of sexual involvement.
- The sexual response cycle is a series of sexual responses; knowledge of this can help you determine your limits.
- Rape is an act of violence; it is illegal.
- Incest is any sexual activity between family members who cannot marry by law.

One area of a dating relationship where good communication is critical is on the level of sexual involvement. First, each person must decide what he or she wants from the relationship. This is not an easy decision, nor is it a one-time decision. It is a decision that you may be faced with repeatedly.

One factor that makes the decision more difficult is the confusion surrounding one's feelings. A person may be experiencing new feelings, such as physical feelings of attraction to another person. These are perfectly normal, healthy feelings. These feelings are caused by hormones and may have nothing to do with being in love with that other person. These feelings are individual and can be triggered by many different circumstances.

Sexual Response

Let's look at the physical response the human body goes through. Our bodies are sensitive to sexual feelings. We may have a physical response to a sexual thought, a scene in a movie, a kiss, holding hands, or the anticipation of an upcoming date with someone special. The heart beats faster, breathing speeds up, hands may get a clammy feeling, and the face gets hot and flushed. In the male, the penis begins to get hard; in the female, vaginal fluid is secreted. These are the body's first responses to excitement. Most of the time these responses stop here.

What is important to know is that these physical responses are normal, and we cannot keep them from happening. When you were 6 years old, you may have giggled at the love scene in a movie, but your body probably did not respond. As a 14- 16-, 26-, or 46-year-old, the presence of the sex hormones causes the body to become excited.

We may not have control over the presence of those feelings, but we do have total control over what we do about them. These feelings do not have to be acted upon. The body can return to its normal state.

However, if a person hasn't clearly decided what he or she wants before getting in a situation where these feelings start to build up, it can become quite difficult to make a responsible decision. A person does not think as clearly when these feelings begin to build. Therefore, it is much easier and smarter to think through a decision about sexual behavior before getting in the situation.

If the excitement continues, the entire body goes through the **sexual response cycle,** a series of sexual responses, which are similar for males and females. Understanding this cycle can help people recognize what is happening to their bodies and determine what limits they wish to set.

The Sexual Response Cycle

Phase One. The first phase of the sexual response cycle is excitement. As it progresses, tension as well as excitement builds. Extra blood from nearby blood vessels flows into spongy tissue in the penis and the walls of the vagina, causing the penis to become hard and the vagina to become wet and its tissue to swell. The clitoris in the female also swells and becomes firm. The female's and male's breasts may also swell slightly.

Phase Two. If the stimulation continues, the body moves into the second phase of response—plateau. Muscles tighten and body tension continues to build.

Both Phase One and Phase Two can last for a few minutes or several hours. Even during the second phase, both the male and female can stop. They do not have to go any further. Obviously, it would become more difficult to stop as the tension builds.

Unfortunately, many decisions about sexual behavior are made in a split second, completely influenced by this physical excitement. A few seconds of continued pleasure can often result in problems later, such as pregnancy, an STD, lowered feelings of self-esteem, and relationship troubles.

If the partners stop at this second phase, they are likely to have a congested, tight feeling in the pelvic area. It may be a dull, aching feeling. This is due to the buildup of blood in the blood vessels. It takes a little while for the body to return to its normal state. It may be uncomfortable, but it is not physically harmful.

Phase Three. During phase three orgasm occurs. During orgasm, the body releases the built-up tension and excitement with a series of muscular contractions that give great pleasure. Most of the time, a male will ejaculate during orgasm. Semen is released from the penis. At the point of ejaculation, there is no turning back or stopping for the male.

The feelings associated with orgasm vary greatly. A person's psychological state can either lessen or heighten the physical response. For example, if the male is worrying about the female's responses, about someone walking in, is feeling guilty about his behavior, or is not in a comfortable position, he may have little feeling. If the female is worrying about doing something wrong, or about getting pregnant, or about her partner's feelings toward her, she may have little feeling. Often, if a person is worried about whether he or she should be doing something, it is a clear sign he or she should not be.

Phase Four. In phase four the body relaxes and returns to its usual state. The swelling in the penis and vagina goes down, pulse and breathing return to normal. This is the resolution phase.

Decisions on Sexual Behavior

There is nothing wrong with young people who decide that they are not ready for a sexual relationship. As a matter of fact, there is a lot that is right with them. Many young people are making this choice. They just don't brag or talk about it in the way others may talk about having sex.

Oftentimes, people who have had sex will pressure their friends to do the same, just to feel better about themselves. Some people who haven't really had sex may boast about imaginary experiences just to impress others.

Why would some people brag about having sex when they haven't?

It is not hard to see why decisions about sexual behavior are so difficult. As you make a decision consider these questions:

- Do I feel any pressure to have sex?
- Am I trying to prove something to someone?
- Am I trying to save this relationship by having sex?
- Have my boyfriend, or girlfriend, and I talked about our expectations in this relationship and how having sex might change the relationship?
- Am I using this person to meet my own needs?
- Am I ready to deal with the possibility of being a parent?
- How would being a parent affect my goals and dreams for the future?
- What would I do if I found out I had an STD?
- What would my parents or family say if they knew I was having sex?
- How would I handle being infected with the AIDS virus?

Let's apply the decision-making process to decisions about having sex.

1. **State the situation that requires a decision.**
   Joel is being pressured by his girlfriend, Amy, to have sex.
2. **List possible choices.**
   a. Joel can tell Amy no, tell her why, and break up with her.
   b. Joel can tell Amy no, tell her why, and continue to date her.
   c. Joel can tell Amy no, tell her why, continue to date her, and also date others.
   d. Joel could have sex with Amy.
3. **Consider the consequences of each possible choice.**
   a. If Joel breaks up with Amy
      —Joel would not have a date for the weekend.
      —Joel no longer has a regular date.
   b. If Joel continues to date Amy
      —Amy could understand Joel's reasons for not having sex and continue dating him.
      —Amy might break up with Joel.
      —Amy could tell their friends Joel will not have sex with her.
   c. If Joel tells Amy no but continues to date her as well as others
      —Amy could understand Joel's reasons, continue dating him, and also date others.

—Amy could break up with Joel and date someone else who will have sex with her.

d. If Joel and Amy had sex,
—one or both of them may like having it.
—one or both of them may not like it.
—Amy could become pregnant.
—either of them could get an STD.
—either of them could become infected with the AIDS virus.
—Amy may not get pregnant or get an STD, including the AIDS virus.
—Joel may not get an STD or infected with the AIDS virus.
—they could feel less close to each other.
—they could feel closer to each other.
—they could feel guilty.
—they may get in trouble with parents.
—they may break up because one or both now feel uncomfortable.
—they may feel that they shouldn't date others.
—they may decide to get married.
—Amy may get a reputation for being easy.
—some guys may want to go out with Amy because she has had sex.
—other guys may hesitate to ask Amy on a date because she has had sex and they feel intimidated or think it was wrong.
—Joel may get a reputation as being too demanding, which may scare off other females from wanting to date him.
—their friends may see them as a serious couple and not include them in group activities.
—they may argue over when, where, and how often to have sex.

4. **Make a decision based on everything you know at this point and act on it.**
   Joel decides to talk with Amy and tell her that he does not want to have sex.
5. **Evaluate your decision.**
   Amy broke up with Joel, but Joel feels good about his decision. After weighing all the possibilities, he knows having sex has consequences that he does not want to deal with. He thinks too many of the consequences have unhealthy results. Too many of the consequences would interfere with the long-range goals he has set for himself.

DID YOU KNOW?

Communication in a relationship can be improved if both persons understand their rights. In any relationship, you have a right to
- make your own decisions.
- ask for what you want.
- be treated with respect.
- say no and not feel guilty.
- express your thoughts and feelings.

Communicating Your Decision

Once people have decided what is best for them, they must communicate that decision clearly. Before getting in the situation, talk to your boyfriend or girlfriend about your decisions. It is not easy to bring up the topic of sex and discuss it. Yet, a couple is much more likely to reach an understanding and grow closer together by trying to talk through this concern.

Saying Yes or No. When do you say yes and when do you say no? When do you move toward the peer group and when do you back away?

These are important decisions that you have probably been faced with and will continue to face. What do you do if your decision goes against what an individual or group is doing? How do you follow your beliefs

Communicate your decisions about how far you want to go on a date.

and not lose face with peers? You can learn to say no by following these simple steps:

- Use your decision-making skills as outlined in Chapter 1.
- If your decision is no, then say no, without feeling you need to justify yourself.
- You will probably be asked to justify why you have refused. This should alert you to the fact that the person asking you has not really accepted your decision, so any explanation will be challenged. Again, you can repeat no.

Here you need to tell yourself that this is a good decision for you, that you will feel better when this pressure is over, and that you will not have to worry about selling yourself out because of others.

- Remember, you may need to repeat yourself several times.
- If the person persists, leave.
- Lastly, avoid compromise if you feel strongly about something. Compromise can be a slow way of saying yes.

WHEN SAYING NO IS NOT ENOUGH

Some people have difficulty accepting no for an answer. When it relates to sex, they may use a variety of lines in response to a no. "You would if you loved me" is probably the most familiar one. Of course, you already know that having sex does not prove anything, especially love. Someone who really loves someone else would not pressure that person to do something he or she was not ready to do.

In his book, *You Would If You Loved Me,* Dr. Sol Gordon, a noted psychologist, suggested some responses to some of the common lines used.

Line	Answer
"I can really turn you on."	"The only thing that needs to be turned on is the lights."
"Everybody else is doing it!"	"That's good. Then I guess you won't have any problem finding someone else."
"Wanna go to bed?"	"No thanks. I just got up."
"You just don't know what you're missing."	"That will make two of us. You won't know what you're missing either.
"Don't worry, I'll use protection."	"You're gonna need protection if you don't leave me alone."
"Want to get in the back seat of my car?"	"No thanks. I'd rather stay up here with you."
"Come on. You know I love you. Let me show you."	"If you did love me, you wouldn't ask."

Remember, good friends will not challenge you to do something that goes against what you believe. They will not try to talk you into doing something you don't want to do.

Sexual Violence

Sometimes relationships go very wrong. One person in the relationship may not believe or listen to someone else's decision not to have sex.

Sex, when forced against a person's will, then becomes an act of violence. Acts of violence involving sexuality are affecting more and more people in our society.

Rape

Rape is sexual intercourse through force or threat of force. Rape is illegal. Rape is not an act of passion; it is an act of violence.

A rape victim can be female or male and someone of any age. It is estimated that one-half million people are raped every year in the United States. In the last few years, incidence of rape has increased by over 40 percent.

Most people think of rape as happening in a dark alley or involving a stranger. Statistics show that 50 percent of all reported rapes happen in the home and most rapists are known by their victims. This can mean recognizing the person as the checker at the local grocery store or a friend.

One in four females under the age of 18 is a victim of rape. Many rapes involving female teens are acquaintance rape or date rape. Aquaintance rape is rape by someone the female knows. Date rape is rape that is done by someone the female is dating. Date rape especially can cause the victim to feel confused, guilty, and ashamed. She may not think of it as rape since she knows the male. Or she may feel responsible if she thinks she didn't say stop soon enough.

Rape is never the victim's fault. Regardless of how well a person knows the rapist, if sex is forced against a person's will, it is rape.

One way to prevent rape from happening again is for all victims to report it. This procedure can be difficult. It may be embarrassing to talk about the rape, but it is the victim's responsibility. If the rape goes unreported, the rapist goes unpunished and will likely rape again. The assailant needs professional intervention.

Avoid situations that put you at risk. What other options could this teen have taken?

Protecting Yourself Against Rape

Perhaps the most important guideline to use in protecting yourself is to employ common sense. Avoid situations where you are putting yourself at risk.

- It is safer to go places with other people.
- If you go alone, tell someone your plans.
- Walk briskly, with purpose and confidence.
- Stay in well-lighted, populated areas.
- Have your keys ready when approaching your home or car.
- Lock all doors and windows in a car and at home. Check inside your car before getting in.
- Never open any door to strangers.
- If you have car trouble, stay locked inside with the windows up. Anyone trying to help will help you best by calling the police.
- If someone is following you or you feel threatened, go to a public place. Run, yell, scream, blow a whistle. Make all the noise you can.
- Try to keep calm and think clearly.
- Drugs and alcohol can make you vulnerable. Do not use them.

Protecting Yourself Against Date Rape

Prevent date rape by:

- Knowing about the person you go out with. Find out who this person's friends are and learn about his or her reputation.
- Making the first few dates ones involving group activities.
- Not spending a lot of time alone or in isolated places.
- Letting someone know where you are going and when you will return.

HEALTH UPDATE

LOOKING AT THE ISSUES

Sexual Harassment

Sexual harassment made big news when, in 1991, University of Oklahoma College of Law Professor Anita Hill accused then Supreme Court nominee Clarence Thomas of this crime.

Many females, and males too, experience sexual harassment at school, in public, or on the job. Sexual harassment takes the form of threats, sexual remarks, obscene jokes, deliberate touching, pressure for dates, letters, calls, assault, or rape. Victims of sexual harassment feel angry and ashamed. Often they may be in a position where the person harassing them has power over them, such as a boss. Unfortunately, some victims do not know their rights or what to do. They fear for their jobs and reputations. The accusation often comes down to one person's word against another's.

Analyzing Different Viewpoints

ONE VIEW. Nothing will happen to a person who sexually harasses another. If a person reports sexual harassment, the person is viewed as a troublemaker or liar. The person this is reported to will not give support anyway. The best thing to do is try to avoid the person who harasses and keep quiet about it.

A SECOND VIEW. In 1980, the Equal Employment Opportunity Commission said that making sexual activity a condition of employment or promotion is a violation of the Civil Rights Act. The Supreme Court agreed in a 1986 case. Most companies now have policies against and procedures to follow to report sexual harassment. Sexual harassment should be reported. The law is on the victim's side.

A THIRD VIEW. People who are harassed are too sensitive and easily offended. There is nothing wrong with complimenting the way someone looks or telling a joke. Most sexual harassment is just fooling around. Others probably do not find the comments offensive.

Exploring Your Views

1. What is your position on the Hill-Thomas controversy?
2. What are situations of sexual harassment you have heard or read about?
3. What can be done to stop sexual harassment?

What to Do if You or Someone You Know Is Raped

If you or someone you know is raped:

- Tell your parent or a close friend. Ask for emotional support.
- Notify the police immediately. Ask for the sex crimes officer, preferably a female officer or advisor who will assist victims.
- Do not take a shower, change clothes, or douche. This is very important since the police will need all the possible evidence they can get.
- Seek a physical examination as soon as possible. A hospital is probably best equipped to care for a rape victim. At the hospital, the following procedures will be necessary:
  - a pelvic examination—this is important for verifying the rape as well as checking for injuries;
  - some hospitals will give the victim an antibiotic to fight possible infections;
  - the nurse or doctor will talk to the victim about possible pregnancy and what can be done.
- Find someone or a support group to help work through the emotional shock of rape. Rape is a very stressful experience. It is only normal that the victim will have a wide range of feelings. Since rape is emotionally harmful, it is important that the victim start the healing process by talking about fears and concerns. Many communities have a rape crisis center with specially trained counselors for this very purpose.

Males as Rape Victims

Most of the attention on rape is given to the female since she is the most common victim. However, male rape is occurring more often. Male rape most often involves another male forcing the victim into a sexual act. Because our society gives males the message that they are strong and should be able to protect themselves, being a male victim of rape may be especially difficult to handle. Shame, embarrassment, and humiliation may keep the victim from telling anyone. This makes coping with the experience even more difficult.

Remember the victim is never at fault. He should call a rape crisis center. These centers have counselors who have dealt with this situation and can help.

A victim of incest should keep telling someone until he or she gets help.

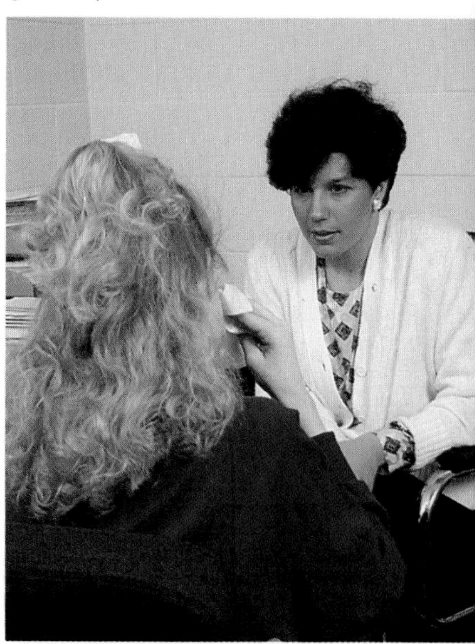

Incest

Incest is any sexual activity between family members who cannot marry by law. It can involve fathers, stepfathers, mothers, stepmothers, uncles, aunts, brothers, sisters, or any relative. The victim may be male or female. Incest is not usually a violent attack. It usually involves persuasion—an adult using his or her power and influence on a child. It may start when the child is young and continue for years. The adult may get the child to promise not to tell or bribe the child into not telling. The adult may say things like:

- "I'll go to jail, and it will be your fault."
- "Others will be very mad at us—they wouldn't understand."
- "This will be our special secret."

Out of fear, loyalty, or obedience the child may say nothing. The child may be further confused if the physical contact with the adult feels good. As a child, he or she may not fully understand that what is being done is wrong.

The most important thing to remember in any case of sexual abuse is the victim is never at fault. It is always the adult's fault. Even though there is little that young people can do to resist, incest victims often feel guilty. They may feel that they caused the incest. This is wrong. Again, it is never the child's fault.

What to Do About Incest

The most important thing a victim of incest can do is to tell someone. This can be very difficult. If the victim goes to another family member, that person may not believe the victim. Some people do not want to face the truth about this kind of problem. They find it easier to deny it. However, the victim should not give up. He or she must find someone else to tell—a school nurse, counselor, a person from church—anyone who can help.

The only way to stop the abuse and get the adult the help needed is to tell someone. Quite often, an adult who abuses children was abused as a child. Such people need help. There are groups now that work with the abusers, as well as the victims of incest. However, the person being abused must first tell someone.

If you have ever been a victim of incest, tell someone. If you know someone who is a victim, encourage him or her to tell someone. However frightening or painful, telling is the first step in doing something about the problem. Remember incest can happen to males as well as females, and it is never the victim's fault.

LESSON 2 REVIEW

Reviewing Facts and Vocabulary

1. Why is it important to make a decision about whether to engage in sex before you get into such a situation?
2. Define *orgasm* and tell what usually accompanies the orgasm in males.
3. Name four of the body's first physiological responses to sexual feelings.
4. List three things you can say or do to refuse to have sex.

Thinking Critically

5. **Evaluation.** What might people think of a high school student who engaged in sexual activity with every person he or she dated? What might you do to help this person?
6. **Synthesis.** Write at least six responses that Dr. Sol Gordon might add to his book entitled, *You Would If You Loved Me.*

Applying Health Knowledge

7. Develop a rape crisis center program. Describe the qualifications of the people you would employ. Include in your program ways to help victims of rape.

CHAPTER 4

Review

Reviewing Facts and Vocabulary

1. List the stages, developed by Elisabeth Kübler-Ross, that a person might go through when losing a loved one to death or when a relationship ends.
2. What are some disadvantages of dating one person exclusively as a teenager?
3. Describe one way in which communication can get mixed up or misunderstood.
4. Is the following statement true or false? "When you are telling someone how you feel, you should always start your statements with the word *you*."
5. Define communication and tell why it is important in dating.
6. From what basic social unit do we mainly form our value system?
7. What effect does change often have on friendships?
8. Why is it important for teenagers to be involved in a variety of social activities?
9. Name one way to decrease the amount of tension and awkwardness of first dates.
10. If someone chooses not to go out with you, should you assume that there is something wrong with you? Explain your answer.
11. How might someone be able to tell that you are a good listener?
12. Define incest and tell who is never at fault in such a situation.

Thinking Critically

13. **Evaluation.** Express your feelings about date rape. Is there ever a situation where the victim is at fault and deserved to be raped? Explain your answer.
14. **Analysis.** Compare a dating relationship you would like to have with one that is not so desirable. Point out the differences and how decisions you make might affect the outcome of the relationship.
15. **Synthesis.** List five bad situations a person might be in that might put him or her at risk of being raped. Suggest ways this person can make better decisions to avoid being raped.
16. **Evaluation.** What do you feel should be punishment for someone who commits incest? Should such a person be punished, helped, or both? Give some suggestions for ways that such a person might be helped.
17. **Synthesis.** Make a chart, listing in the left column, ten values that are important to you. These might include honesty, loyalty, and working hard. In the right column, tell what experiences or people helped form these values that are important to you.

Applying Health Knowledge

18. Imagine a close family member has come to you and said he wanted to tell you something very personal. He makes you promise not to say anything to anyone. He continues to tell you that he was raped by another family member. Considering that this person's life and health may depend upon the decisions you make to help handle the situation, how can you best help this person?

Beyond the Classroom

19. **Parental Involvement.** Discuss with your parents some important values that you learned from them. Make a list of at least ten more values that you feel would be important to teach your own children some day. Ask your parents for suggestions and advice about ways you could teach values to your future family.
20. **Further Study.** Do research at the library and talk to doctors about treatment for victims of rape and incest. Write a report about the treatment process and add suggestions that you personally feel might help victims. Suggest ways that present treatment might be improved.

CHAPTER

5

Marriage and Parenthood

LESSON 1

THE COMMITMENT TO MARRY

A **commitment** is an agreement or a pledge to do something in the future. Think of some commitments you have made—perhaps to babysit, work on decorations for a school function, or get your family's groceries. Making a commitment and carrying through with the agreement or promise helps build trust in a relationship. It also helps develop a sense of personal responsibility.

One of the most serious life commitments a person can make is a commitment to marriage. When a person chooses to marry, he or she is making a commitment to share life with another person. Obviously, such a commitment should not be taken lightly. However, many people, though they take the decision to marry seriously, do not consider its lifelong impact.

At least 90 percent of all Americans marry at some time in their lives. Some people may feel pressure to marry. Before people make such a major life decision, they must clearly identify their motives for marrying if they expect to be successful.

LESSON 1 FOCUS

TERMS TO USE

- Commitment
- Blended family

CONCEPTS TO LEARN

- There are both positive and negative reasons people marry.
- Divorce causes many changes for family members.

Reasons for Marrying

If a person is getting married because of social pressure, it might be wise to reconsider. If a person is considering marriage to escape problems at home, because the female is pregnant, or to prove a point, he or she is starting out on very shaky ground. With current statistics indicating that over one-half of all marriages end in divorce, such a start is cause for real concern.

Most people say they are marrying because they are in love, and on a surface level, that may be true. Often, however, other motives may be hidden deeply inside. Without close self-examination, a person may not even be aware of them. Other people may be aware of these motives but may not be willing to admit them. If a person has any doubt or questions about reasons for getting married or about the person that he or she is marrying, the best time to reconsider is before the marriage.

The Marital Relationship

"But we are in love." The idea of romantic love is very glamorized in our society today. Countless movies and books portray the Romeo and Juliet type of romance. These stories are full of passion and excitement and usually end happily ever after.

Unfortunately, such stories present an inaccurate picture of relationships. Almost all relationships do begin with romantic love, physical attraction, and an atmosphere of excitement and energy between the two individuals. Many couples are successful in maintaining this romantic side of their relationship.

However, all relationships go through various stages. When the first stage of newness and excitement settles, the couple must look closely to see how well they get along with each other on a day-to-day basis. This includes seeing the other person when not at his or her best. Unfortunately, many young couples make decisions about marriage based on the romantic phase of their relationship.

Two factors critical to a successful marriage are emotional and social maturity. Perhaps the most important factor in being mature is that a person is aware of his or her emotional needs and how to meet them in healthy ways.

How does this point affect the success of a marriage? The marriage has a better chance of being successful if both individuals have worked out beforehand healthy ways to meet their emotional needs. Each has friends, belongs to a group, and is in some way making a contribution in life; that is, each feels worthwhile. Then both individuals will not go into a marriage depending only on the marriage or the spouse to fully meet these needs.

As you can see, a person must consider many complex areas before getting married. Knowing a future spouse is, of course, very important to the success of a marriage. However, knowing yourself—your innermost thoughts, feelings, fears, and dreams—is perhaps the most critical element for making a marriage work.

Factors Affecting Marital Adjustment

Sociologists have conducted extensive research to develop measures of marital adjustment. In one study of over 7,000 couples, two researchers concluded that a well-adjusted marriage was one in which the husband and wife:

In a well-adjusted marriage, common interests are shared.

1. agreed on critical issues in their relationship,
2. shared common interests and activities,
3. demonstrated affection and shared confidences,
4. had few complaints about the marriage,
5. did not have feelings of loneliness or irritability.

The researchers went further to identify a number of social background factors associated with successful marital adjustment. Some of the more significant factors included:

- similarity in family backgrounds,
- domestic happiness of their parents,
- lack of conflict with parents (in-laws),
- increased educational achievement for both spouses,
- having several friends of both sexes and belonging to organizations,
- having a long period of close association prior to marriage,
- having security and stability of occupation (this was more important than income),
- agreement on whether to have children.

These factors were even more significant when combined. That is, the more factors both partners have experienced, the better the marital adjustment.

Marriage and Divorce

Over the past few years, we have seen a change in marital patterns. People are waiting a little longer before they get married. In the United States, the average age to marry is the mid-20s for both males and females. After seeing the divorce rate soar, we are now seeing a slight decrease in divorce. Yet, we still have an alarming divorce rate; over 50 percent of marriages end in divorce.

Divorce causes many changes. The family is physically separated. At least one member of the family moves and has new living arrangements. Children may feel they will miss out on many experiences by not growing up with both parents. In addition, if children move, they may attend a new school and will have to make new friends. The availability of finances is another change. In many cases of divorce, fewer funds are available to the family when the parents split up. All of these changes, as well as a loss of day-to-day parental support can cause emotional stress.

The divorce of parents can be very upsetting for children. It is often hard for them to understand. Many children blame themselves for their parents' troubles. This, of course, is wrong. It is not the children's fault, but they may have difficulty understanding that. Divorce upsets the children's routine and can threaten their sense of security. Emotional wounds can last a long time.

For these reasons, parents should make every effort to reassure the child and not to involve the child in the adults' disagreements. Unfortunately, if the parents are emotionally upset or having trouble coping themselves, they may overlook the child's needs.

There is no easy answer when a family goes through a divorce. There are places both parents and children can go for help—and to talk with someone about their feelings. It is especially important for young people to find someone they can trust to talk with and to help them through the difficult times.

DID YOU KNOW?

- Married people are found to be physically and mentally healthier than single, divorced, separated, or widowed, people.
- Healthier people are more likely to marry and stay married.
- The average age for marriage in the United States is almost 26 for males and 24 for females.

Blended Families

Most people who get divorced will remarry. Many of those who do remarry will have children living with them. When an adult, or adults, with children marry, families are blended. A **blended family** is a family that is formed when two adults marry and have children from a previous marriage or marriages living with them. Children from blended families often acquire new relatives when a parent remarries. These relatives include a stepparent and, in most cases, stepbrothers, stepsisters, and/or step-grandparents. Children from blended families may also have halfbrothers and/or halfsisters, siblings that share one biological parent.

Whenever two families come to live together, there are going to be changes. These changes can be stressful. Children and teenagers who were used to having their parent to themselves now find that they are sharing the parent's attention. They may even be sharing the house they have lived in for years with other children. It is normal to feel a variety of emotions, such as jealousy, anger, or sadness. It is important to look for healthy ways to express these feelings. Again, talking with someone the child or teen can trust is healthier than keeping it all inside.

Change is inevitable when two families are brought together to live in one house.

Teenage Marriage—A Risky Commitment

Although some teenage marriages do work, three out of four end in divorce. The teenage years are an important period of development. Since young people are just beginning to establish their own identities, it is unlikely that they are ready to make a choice of, or lifelong commitment to, a marriage partner.

In centuries past, young people 12 to 14 years old married and quickly had children. This was encouraged in order to provide workers and ensure the continuation of the family. The average life expectancy of a person 100 years ago was between 45 and 60 years, so the life cycle was short. Infant mortality also was very high.

Today, because of better nutrition and modern medicine, people live longer. With the current need for a good education to get a job, people must spend more time training for a career. This training can continue into a person's 20s.

Marrying in the teens, therefore, has more negatives than positives:

- Such early marriage can interfere with the teenager's personal growth and development. Many times, a young person gives up his or her personal interests and goals to direct attention to the marriage. This can result in unfulfilled, unhappy individuals. It may be difficult for the teenage couple to grow together and maintain a common bond.
- Finances also present a problem for teenage marriage. If the partners have not finished high school, their earning power is severely limited. Trying to finish school and work at the same time puts great stress on the individuals. A young person may not yet have the skills to cope with such stress. As frustration builds, he or she may begin to take it out on the spouse.
- One of the main reasons for teenage marriage is an unexpected pregnancy. Getting married under this condition puts even greater financial and emotional stress on the marriage.

It is possible for a teenage marriage to be successful. However, it is an exception rather than a norm.

LESSON 1 REVIEW

Reviewing Facts and Vocabulary

1. Define commitment, and name three commitments that you have made.
2. List three bad reasons for deciding to get married.
3. Name three factors that affect marital adjustment.
4. Explain the meaning of a blended family.

Thinking Critically

5. **Analysis.** Why is a portrayal of marriage from a novel, TV, or movie often unrealistic?
6. **Evaluation.** When do you feel someone can know that they are ready to get married?

Applying Health Knowledge

7. Study your local newspaper for one week to find out how many marriages and divorces occur within that week. Discuss your findings with your class.

Becoming a Parent

Without question, having a child requires tremendous marital adjustments. Rearing children is probably the most difficult job one can have. It is certainly one for which we are not usually prepared. A couple should give much consideration to this decision, since it has a significant impact on personal health and, thus, the health of their relationship.

LESSON 2 FOCUS

Terms to Use
- Heredity

Concepts to Learn
- There are many reasons for having children.
- Becoming a parent as a teen affects physical, mental, and social health.

Why People Have Children

Couples give many reasons for having children. Some of these reasons include:

- bringing stability to a shaky marriage,
- passing on the family name and **heredity,** genetic characteristics passed from parent to child,
- giving one's parents a grandchild,
- having someone to be loved by,
- giving in to pressure from friends and parents,
- wanting to make a family complete,
- wanting to love a child.

Does it surprise you that one of the least mentioned reasons that parents give for having a child is a love for children? Sometimes the reasons for having a child may make the adjustment to parenthood a difficult one. A child is a full-time responsibility. If there were marital problems before the child, these problems are likely to increase with the birth of a baby.

Communicating becomes even more important when a child joins the family. The parents must make important decisions about how the child will be reared and how household tasks will be divided, especially if both parents work outside the home.

Parental Responsibilities

Parents are the most important teachers a child will ever have. They are responsible for the child's physical, emotional, social, and intellectual development and well-being—a task that requires much time and thought. It is, or should be, the parents' goal to rear a responsible, healthy, independent person.

What can parents do to successfully achieve this goal? First, it is important that parents maintain their own health. A parent should not neglect his or her needs in the process of caring for a child. A parent will not function well if he or she is tired, irritable, or pressed for time.

Second, parents need to get away by themselves for short periods of time to relax and enjoy a day or evening out. The parent must keep his or her mental and physical stamina at a healthy level.

DID YOU KNOW?

- Rearing children is costly. The cost of a college education can put families in great debt. According to The College Board, a child entering college in the year 2000 will need from $33,000 to $45,000 to complete 4 years at a state college and $120,000 to complete 4 years at a private institution.

ARE YOU READY TO BECOME A PARENT?

Decide whether the statements below describe you. Would you consider yourself ready to become a parent?

- Physically I am mature enough to have a healthy pregnancy. (females only)
- Emotionally I am ready for a pregnancy.
- I am ready to give up much of my freedom to take on the responsibilities of parenthood.
- I have met my educational goals.
- I like children and have had some experience around them.
- I have a lot of patience, especially around children.
- When I get angry, I express my emotions in a healthy manner.
- Having a baby now fits in with my personal life goals.
- I feel good about myself.
- I am capable of giving a baby the love and attention he or she needs.
- I have a husband or wife who is supportive of me and willing to help with a baby.
- I am aware of the expense involved in rearing a child.
- I have the financial means of providing for a family.
- I know what to expect of a child at various developmental ages.

Teen Parenthood

Consider the basic tasks of adolescence discussed in Chapter 2. Think about everything that goes on in a teen's life as he or she works toward achieving those tasks. During this time, you grow in many ways. You are given more freedom and spend more time with friends. This can be a very enjoyable time of life. You could say that being a teenager is a full-time job. What impact does becoming a parent have on a teen's healthy growth and development?

Wanting to love a child is a great reason to have one.

A Teen Parent's Physical Health

The adolescent female's body is still growing, and thus, is not yet fully mature. Pregnancy presents a serious health risk to a teenager and her baby. Teens are less likely to receive early prenatal care and may not have a well-balanced, healthy diet. These are some of the reasons babies born to teens are more likely to have lower birth weights. The lower the birth weight, the greater the chances are for developmental problems. Risks of complications during childbirth are greater for teens than for older females in their 20s or 30s. In addition, teens experience a greater number of miscarriages. A miscarriage is the body's expulsion of a human fetus.

A Teen Parent's Mental and Social Health

The problems described under physical health will also impact a teenager's mental and/or social health. Pregnancy is the most common cause of dropping out of school for both males and females. Without a high school diploma, job opportunities are very limited. As a result, earning potential is very low. The younger a person is when he or she becomes a parent, the greater are the chances of living in poverty. Not being able to provide for one's family can negatively affect mental health and cause a poor self-concept and stress.

Becoming a teenage parent more than likely means missing much of the socializing that is important during the teenage years. The 24-hour-a-day demands of a baby make it difficult to find time and healthy ways for the parent to meet his or her emotional needs. The teenage parent can feel very alone. This situation can lead to frustration and anger. Add to the fact that most teens have had no preparation for this new role as a parent. It is not hard to understand why these young parents become frustrated. The younger the parents are, the greater the chances of child abuse and neglect.

Dreams and goals change when taking responsibility for someone else.

HEALTH UPDATE

LOOKING AT THE ISSUES

Paying Child Support

As part of a divorce settlement, financial arrangements are usually set up so provisions for children, and sometimes spouses, continue after the divorce.

Unfortunately some fathers choose to no longer support their children financially. Going to court to get the support is timely and costly to both sides. Some attorneys are trying to fight harder against these problems. They are doing this by going after delinquent parents with felony charges to get the money that is due. Felony charges carry larger financial penalties and longer prison terms than do misdemeanor charges. Faced with such long prison terms, many males work to make good on their financial obligations. When they don't, the children suffer the most. They may suffer not only because of lack of financial support but also because they still love their dad.

Analyzing Different Viewpoints

ONE VIEW. Charging these fathers with felonies is fair. The father is aware of his obligations and should honor them, especially for the children's sake.

A SECOND VIEW. Many fathers are hurting financially. They often have new families to care for. Most females work today, and should be equally responsible for the children's financial obligations.

Exploring Your Views

1. What is your opinion about serving these delinquent fathers with felony charges?
2. If you were a judge, how would you rule in a case like this?
3. What other options might be available to encourage these fathers to pay?
4. How much should the parent who has custody be expected to financially handle?

The Teen Father

A lot of attention is given to the pregnant teenage female. There also is increasing information about and for the teenage father. The father's responsibility of caring for a child cannot be taken lightly. How does becoming a father affect a male teen? An unplanned pregnancy can be a very stressful experience for the teen male. He will encounter major changes in his life. As discussed earlier, pregnancy is the primary cause for dropping out of school. Many teen fathers need to quit school in order to go to work to help financially support a child. However, without a high school diploma, job opportunities for them will be limited. Free time with friends will be limited as other responsibilities take priority.

Some communities have programs that help teen fathers learn how to be a good parent. However, before becoming a parent, males need to make personal decisions about sex and consider the consequences of their actions.

Deciding When Not to Become a Parent

Unplanned pregnancies can be prevented. Couples should talk to each other about their goals in life and what steps need to be taken to meet those goals. Couples also need to discuss what they expect out of their relationship. Each person must decide what he or she wants in the relationship. If either of you is not ready to become a parent, remember that the only 100 percent effective method of preventing pregnancy is not having sexual intercourse. Nothing is wrong with a male or female who decides he or she is not ready to have sexual intercourse. No one has a right to pressure a person to do something he or she is not ready to do. It is not only okay to say no, it is a person's right. For teenagers, it is the most healthy choice.

LESSON 2 REVIEW

Reviewing Facts and Vocabulary

1. List reasons people have children.
2. What is a common reason males and females drop out of high school? How does this fact affect their financial situation?
3. Explain why pregnancy presents a serious health risk to a teenager and her baby.

Thinking Critically

4. **Synthesis.** What stressful situations might a teenager experience as a result of an unexpected pregnancy?
5. **Evaluation.** What do you think are the two most important responsibilities of being a parent?

Applying Health Knowledge

6. Babysit or observe some children, preferably under the age of five. List characteristics you find unique to the age group of the children you watch. List behaviors they exhibit that might be difficult to handle.

CHAPTER 5

REVIEW

Reviewing Facts and Vocabulary

1. About what percentage of marriages in the United States end in divorce?
2. About what percentage of Americans marry at some time in their lives?
3. Tell which of the following is not a factor affecting marital adjustment:
   a. A husband and wife like to do the same kinds of things in their spare time.
   b. A husband and wife both wear the same size clothing.
   c. A husband and wife both enjoy being married.
4. Name two adjustments a teenage male may have to make if he unexpectedly becomes a parent.
5. What is the only sure way to prevent pregnancy until a person is ready to become a parent?
6. How can a female teen's physical health be affected by pregnancy?
7. Name four reasons someone might have children.
8. Name four social background factors that can affect marital success.

Thinking Critically

9. **Evaluation.** On what factors will you base your decision as to whether you will be ready for marriage or whether you will choose to marry at all?
10. **Synthesis.** Considering the factors that make up a successful marriage, what might be some reasons that marriages end in divorce?
11. **Analysis.** Make a comparison between a strong marriage and a weak marriage that you see occurring in your family or community. Without using names, tell what characteristics make up each kind of marriage.
12. **Evaluation.** Why do you think some people make better parents than others? State reasons for your opinion.
13. **Evaluation.** Offer some solutions to teen pregnancy.

Applying Health Knowledge

14. Make a FOR and an AGAINST list concerning marriage and children. Give reasons someone should get married and reasons he or she should not get married. Use the same process concerning whether to have children.

Beyond the Classroom

15. **Parental Involvement.** Discuss the following statement with your parents: Three out of four teenage marriages end in divorce and the younger a person is when he or she becomes a parent, the greater are the chances of living in poverty. Find out how your parents feel about this, and what guidance they can give you concerning these issues.
16. **Community Involvement.** Check with a local church or social agency about ways that you might be of assistance to a teenage couple facing an unexpected pregnancy. You may be able to help a female teenager who is pregnant and needs assistance. Discuss your experience with your family and classmates.
17. **Community Involvement.** Call your public health department to ask where couples can go for genetic counseling. Get names and phone numbers. Call one or more of the numbers to learn what services are available. Make a written report and discuss your findings with the class.
18. **Community Involvement.** List at least three places in your community where a woman can go for a pregnancy test.
19. **Community Involvement.** Find out whether any hospitals in your area have nurse-midwife delivery programs. Learn the details of such programs.

CHAPTER 6

PREGNANCY AND CHILDBIRTH

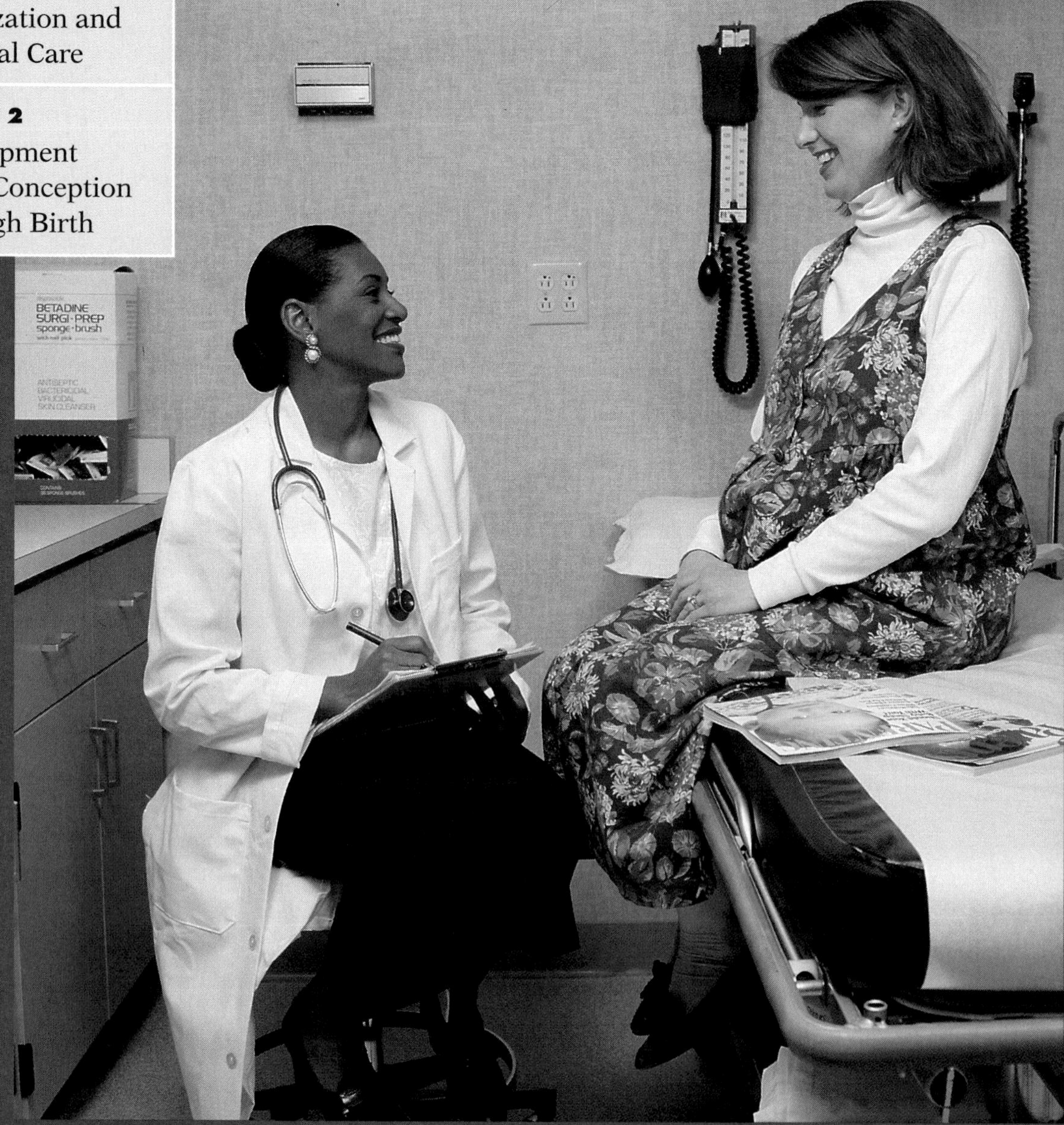

Fertilization and Prenatal Care

The majority of couples who marry will choose to have children. There are many responsibilities to consider before becoming a parent. Parents need to be prepared to provide for the physical, mental, and social well-being of a child.

As soon as a male begins to produce sperm, he becomes capable of fathering a child. As soon as a female begins to ovulate, she becomes capable of becoming pregnant. A female can actually become pregnant before she starts to menstruate. Remember that menstruation occurs because the ovum is not fertilized. If an ovum is fertilized, there is no menstrual period.

LESSON 1 FOCUS

Terms to Use

- Zygote
- Blastocyst
- Embryo
- Amnion
- Placenta
- Umbilical cord
- Fetal alcohol syndrome

Concepts to Learn

- Pregnancy begins with the union of an ovum and a sperm cell.
- A baby develops during many stages of cell division.
- Prenatal care includes regular checkups, a well-balanced diet, and not using illegal drugs, drinking alcohol, or using tobacco.

Fertilization

Pregnancy begins with the union of an ovum from the mother and a sperm cell from the father. During sexual intercourse, the erect penis is placed in the vagina. Hundreds of millions of sperm are released during ejaculation and immediately begin swimming into the uterus and then into each Fallopian tube. If an ovum is present in the Fallopian tube, one sperm can fertilize the ovum. A fertilized ovum is called a **zygote.** A film immediately surrounds the zygote, preventing any other sperm from penetrating it. The remaining sperm cells die. Fertilization usually takes place in the upper one-third of a Fallopian tube.

An ectopic pregnancy occurs when the fertilized ovum cell implants outside the uterus. Although the fertilized ovum may implant at various places in the reproductive system of the female, the most common site of ectopic pregnancy is in one of the Fallopian tubes. An ectopic pregnancy, if not diagnosed early and treated, could be fatal to the mother.

Days 3 to 4

The zygote now begins its journey to the uterus. This takes about three to four days. The process of cell division has already begun. When a cavity forms in the center of these cells, the cells are called a **blastocyst.** By the end of the pregnancy, the fertilized ovum will have divided millions of times.

Days 4 to 5

The blastocyst spends another few days in the uterus, preparing to implant in the uterine lining. During this time, it receives nourishment from the secretions of this lining. Since the beginning of the menstrual cycle, the lining of the uterus has been preparing to receive the fertilized ovum. This lining is called the endometrium. It becomes thick and spongy to prepare for implantation of the fertilized ovum.

Beginning at the top left corner, these photos show the unfertilized ovum; a sperm penetrating an ovum; the zygote within a protective shield. Bottom row, left to right: a two-cell zygote; an eight-cell zygote; and a blastocyst.

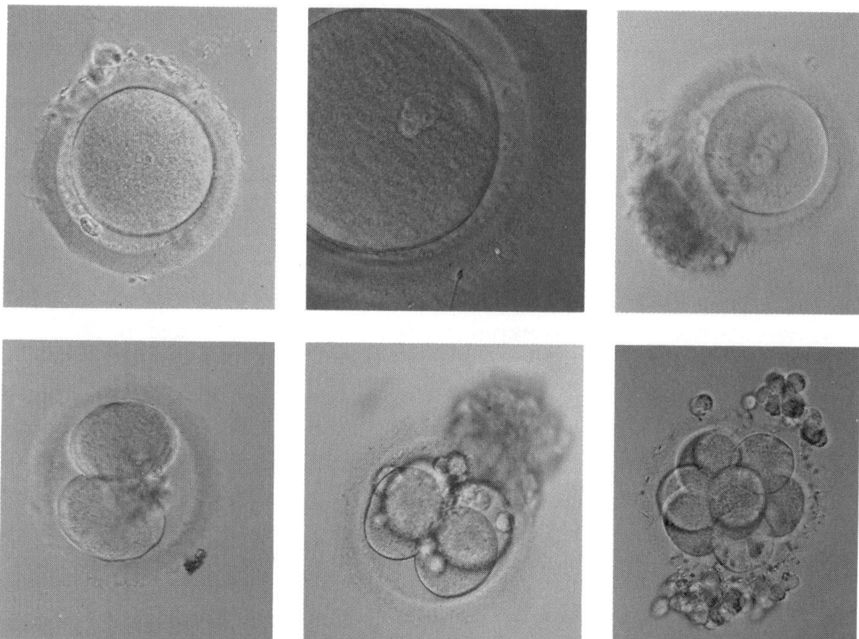

Days 7 to 8

Finally, about seven to eight days after fertilization, the blastocyst attaches to the inner wall of the uterus. Now it produces special enzymes, complex proteins that cause chemical reactions, to aid the blastocyst in dissolving some of the uterine lining. Gradually, the blastocyst becomes buried within the lining. This process is called implantation. The implanted blastocyst is now called an **embryo.** At this point, the embryo is in the first stages of development. Now, it is about the size of the dot over an *i.*

The Embryo, Placenta, and Umbilical Cord

The cells of the developing embryo continue to divide until three layers form the baby's organs. One layer becomes the respiratory and digestive systems. One layer develops into muscles, bones, blood vessels, and skin. The third layer becomes the nervous system, sense organs, and mouth.

Special membranes also form around the developing embryo. One of these membranes forms a fluid-filled sac around the embryo called the **amnion,** or bag of waters. This developing sac acts like a shock absorber, providing a moist cushion that protects the embryo.

The **placenta** is a structure that forms along the lining of the uterus as the embryo implants. It is made of blood-rich tissue that transfers oxygen and nutrients from the mother's blood to the embryo's blood. The placenta has several jobs, serving as lungs, liver, kidneys, endocrine glands, and digestive system for the developing embryo. The embryo is connected to the placenta by the **umbilical cord.** The umbilical cord grows to a length of about 20 inches.

Blood vessels from the embryo connect to blood vessels that go through the umbilical cord and into the placenta. The mother's blood vessels also extend into the placenta. The blood of the mother and that of the embryo never mix. However, the blood vessels come close enough

DID YOU KNOW?

- On July 25, 1978, the birth of a 5-pound, 12-ounce healthy baby girl in an English hospital made medical history. Louise Brown became the first baby ever to be born as a result of in vitro fertilization. The term *in vitro* literally means "in glass." In vitro fertilization refers to fertilization of an egg by a sperm outside of the body or in an artificial environment. After fertilization, the developing embryo is implanted in the female's uterus.

to allow oxygen and nutrients to enter the embryo's bloodstream. In the same manner, waste products leave the embryo's blood and are removed from the mother's body. About three-fourths of a quart of the mother's blood travels through the placenta each minute.

A new hormone, human chorionic gonadotropin, or HCG, is now secreted by the placenta. This hormone stimulates the production and release of greater amounts of estrogen and progesterone, which help maintain the lining of the uterus, keeping it suitable for pregnancy. These hormones also prevent the ovaries from releasing any more ova. Thus, another ovum cannot be fertilized once one pregnancy has begun.

DID YOU KNOW?

- A female can get pregnant without having intercourse. If sperm are left on the outside of her body near the vagina, they can move into the vagina. Even if the hymen, the thin membrane covering the opening of the vagina in some females is intact, sperm can move through the small openings in the hymen.

Determining Pregnancy

Pregnancy tests are based on testing the urine for the presence of HCG. Small amounts of HCG are cleansed from the blood through the mother's kidneys. So HCG can be detected in the urine as early as the first week after a missed menstrual period. Doctors can also perform a test known as radioimmunoassay. It can detect HCG in urine or blood as early as a week before the menstrual period is to begin. The doctor will also do an internal examination to further confirm pregnancy. Changes in the cervix and size of the uterus are observed when a female is pregnant.

Home Pregnancy Tests

There are several home pregnancy tests on the market today. These test urine for the presence of HCG in a way similar to how a doctor would conduct the test. However, in one study of these tests, negative results were found to be less reliable than positive test results. A person who uses a home test and has a negative result might not confirm the results at a doctor's office or clinic. If the home test was not accurate, the female may miss early prenatal care and may be making choices that are not good for her baby's health.

Home pregnancy tests should be confirmed by a doctor.

DID YOU KNOW?

- In most case of twins, the female's ovaries release two mature eggs instead of one. When separate sperm cells fertilize each egg cell, two embryos develop. The two embryos, called fraternal twins, have different genetic makeup and, therefore, do not look any more alike than brothers and sisters normally do.
- In other cases, after one egg cell has been fertilized, it divides and two embryos develop. These embryos have the same genetic information and, therefore, are identical twins.

A Girl or a Boy?

Will a baby be a girl or a boy? Of the 46 chromosomes in a fertilized ovum, two are specialized sex chromosomes. In females, these two chromosomes look exactly alike and are called X chromosomes. In males, one chromosome is shorter and does not match the other. Geneticists, scientists who study genetics (the process of heredity), call the smaller one the Y chromosome.

Remember that sperm and ova contain only half the number of chromosomes as other cells. This means that these cells contain only one sex chromosome, not two. Sperm cells may contain either an X or a Y chromosome. An ovum carries an X chromosome. If an ovum is fertilized by a sperm cell carrying an X chromosome, the baby is a girl because, as the chromosomes pair, the combination is XX. If the sperm cell is carrying a Y chromosome, the pairing forms an XY combination, resulting in a boy. So the determination of the sex of a child is based on the father's sperm cell.

Prenatal Care

The sooner the mother confirms her pregnancy, the sooner she can begin prenatal care. This is important because the mother's health choices affect the developing baby's health. A pregnant female should have regular visits with an obstetrician, a doctor specializing in the care of a female and her developing baby.

The obstetrician gives the pregnant female a complete physical examination, including blood tests and a pelvic examination. The obstretrician also monitors the developing baby. Possible complications may be identified at this time and, in some cases, corrected early. The doctor will discuss important health behaviors with the mother. Her eating habits are a special concern. She needs a well-balanced diet to ensure proper nourishment not only for herself but also for her developing baby.

This boy has brain damage due to fetal alcohol syndrome. Fetal alcohol syndrome does not have to happen.

The doctor may also discuss the importance of exercise during pregnancy. Depending on the mother's health and level of fitness, the doctor will have recommendations for a safe exercise program. The doctor will also monitor the female's weight during pregnancy.

A pregnant female must be very careful about what substances she puts in her body. She should not take any medicine without her doctor's permission. She should not use illegal drugs, drink alcohol, or use tobacco.

Alcohol and Pregnancy

Females who drink alcohol during pregnancy run a high risk of giving birth to babies who show physical, mental, and behavioral abnormalities and birth defects. This condition is called **fetal alcohol syndrome.** Babies who are born with this syndrome are shorter and lighter in weight than babies born to mothers who did not drink alcohol. These babies can have a variety of problems. These include impaired speech, a cleft palate, general weakness, slow body growth, facial abnormalities, poor coordination, and heart defects. Mental retardation, poor attention span, nervousness, and hyperactivity also are common.

The alcohol that the mother takes in is passed into her blood and flows through the vessels in the umbilical cord into the blood of the unborn infant. If the mother drinks enough, the baby becomes drunk. A baby born to a female who drinks alcohol during her pregnancy can be born addicted to alcohol.

Unfortunately, the developing infant cannot rid the body of alcohol as an adult can, therefore the alcohol remains in the infant's body much longer. If this heavy drinking is done on a weekly basis, chances are that the unborn infant never fully rids its body of alcohol. The unborn infant cannot say no when it has had enough.

Fetal alcohol syndrome is completely preventable. It does not occur in nondrinking pregnant females. Every female who is pregnant has the choice not to drink.

Smoking and Pregnancy

A pregnant female also should avoid smoking cigarettes. Babies born to females who smoke have a greater chance of being born premature and thus have lower birth weights. Babies with low birth weights of 5½ pounds (2.3 k) or less often develop serious health problems early in life. In fact, low birth weight is the leading cause of death in the first year of life. Some low birth weight babies later have learning problems in school. Pregnant females who smoke are about two times more likely to have a miscarriage or stillbirth than mothers who do not smoke. There also are dangers to unborn babies from passive smoke.

LESSON 1 REVIEW

Reviewing Facts and Vocabulary

1. Define *zygote* and tell what happens to the zygote within the first four days after fertilization.
2. Describe the important function of the amnion.
3. Which of the following statements is not true of the placenta:
   - **a.** The placenta serves as the lungs and digestive system for the developing embryo.
   - **b.** The umbilical cord connects the embryo to the placenta.
   - **c.** The placenta forms along the lining of the Fallopian tubes.
4. What two things might a doctor do to determine if a female is pregnant?
5. Does the father's sperm or the mother's ova determine the sex of the baby?

Thinking Critically

6. **Synthesis.** How might prenatal care make a difference in the development of the baby and in the health of the mother?
7. **Evaluation.** Do you think a female should be charged with a crime if she willingly drinks alcohol or takes illegal drugs during her pregnancy?

Applying Health Knowledge

8. Contact the March of Dimes and find out what birth defects can be prevented. Make a chart showing ways that these birth defects can be prevented and present it to your class.

Development From Conception Through Birth

LESSON 2 FOCUS

Terms to Use

- Fetus
- Ultrasound
- Amniocentesis
- Episiotomy
- Postpartum period
- Caesarean birth
- Birthing centers
- Birth defects

Concepts to Learn

- Tests performed during pregnancy verify if a baby is at risk or if a problem is present.
- There are three stages of labor.
- Parents-to-be can choose from many childbirth options.

During the first 6 weeks of pregnancy, the embryo grows rapidly. At the start of the sixth week, it is 1 millimeter long, or about 10,000 times the size of the original ovum. It already contains millions of cells that are arranging themselves into tissues and organs.

The brain is one of the first organs to develop. Neurons appear around the eighteenth day after fertilization. Three weeks later, the rapidly growing central nervous system causes the head to take shape.

When the embryo is 56 days old and measures about 1 inch (2.5 cm) in length, it enters the second phase of its development. From the eighth week until birth, it is known as a **fetus.** Beneath its transparent, hairless skin—which is covered by a waxy, protective coating—the fetus has all of its major organs and tissues, although they are very tiny. During the remaining 32 weeks, until birth, the fetus will increase in length 12½ times, and its organs will increase 120 times in weight.

Genetic Testing Prior to Pregnancy

Genetic counseling is a process in which the genetic histories of the male and female are studied to predict or determine the presence of certain inherited diseases. Certain tests help prospective parents know of the probability of passing inherited diseases on to their child.

For example, 1 in 12 Black people in the United States carries a single gene for sickle-cell anemia and has the sickle-cell trait. If both parents have the trait, each of their children has a 1 in 4 chance of having sickle-cell anemia. If one of the parents has the trait and the other has sickle-cell anemia, each child will have a 50 percent chance of having the disease. The couple can make an informed decision about having children if they have testing prior to pregnancy.

Tay-Sachs disease is another example of a genetic disease whose presence can be tested. Though rare in the general population, Tay-Sachs is more common in Jewish people of Eastern European origin. People of this origin may wish to be tested for the trait prior to deciding whether to have children. Tay-Sachs results in severe brain dysfunction, paralysis, blindness, and death, which can occur at an early age.

Rh Factor in Blood

The Rh factor is a substance in the blood. About 86 percent of us have an Rh antigen in our red blood cells and are called Rh+. Those who do not have it are Rh−. If someone with Rh− receives transfusions containing Rh+, the Rh− blood gradually builds up antibodies to defend the blood from the Rh antigen. This causes some red blood cells to break down and their products to spread throughout the body. Mixing Rh factors in the blood causes blood cells to mass together. This can cause serious complications. Every Rh− female should have her blood checked regularly, beginning early in pregnancy. If she has received an Rh+ blood transfusion or if the father is Rh+, there could be problems when the antibodies from the mother cross the placenta and attack the baby's red blood cells. Fortunately a serum called Rhogain can be given to the Rh- mother to prevent the build-up of antibodies.

Stages of development before birth (a) 6 weeks; (b) 2 months; (c) 4 months; and (d) 5 to 6 months.

DEVELOPMENT IN THE WOMB BEFORE BIRTH

End of First Month
- One-quarter inch (6 mm) long
- Heart, brain, and lungs forming
- Heart starts beating on about the 25th day

End of Second Month
- About 1.5 inches (3.8 cm) long
- Muscles, skin developing
- Arms, hands, and fingers forming
- Legs beginning to form, along with knees, ankles, and toes
- Every vital organ starting to develop

End of Third Month
- About 3 inches (7.5 cm) long
- Weighs about 1 ounce (28.3 g)
- Movement can be felt
- Can open and close mouth and swallow

End of Fourth Month
- 8 to 10 inches (20 to 25 cm) long
- Weighs 6 ounces (169.8 g)

End of Fifth Month
- About 12 inches (30 cm) long
- Weighs 1 pound (453.6 g)
- Eyelashes appear
- Nails begin to grow
- Heartbeat can be heard

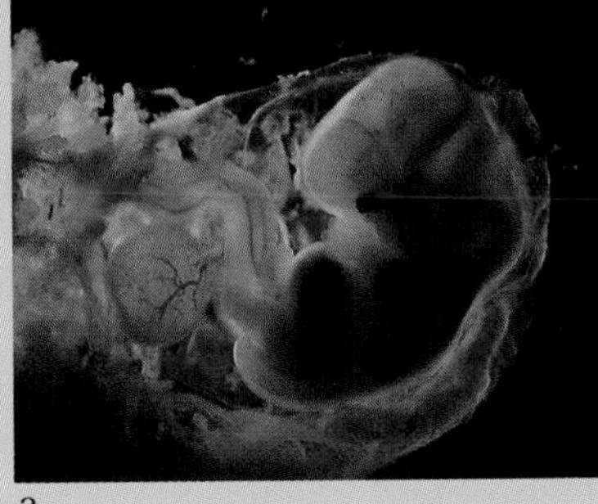
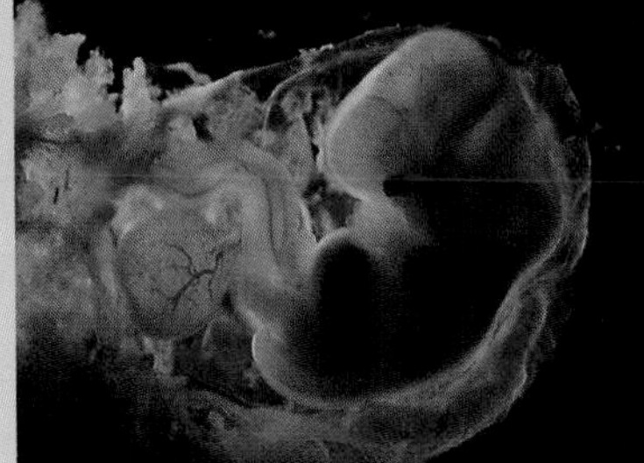

a.

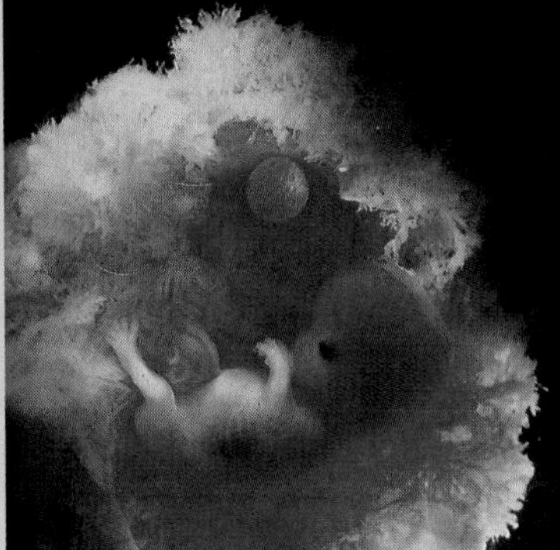

b.

End of Sixth Month
- Can kick and cry
- Can hear sounds
- Might even hiccup
- Has fingernails and footprints

End of Seventh Month
- Weighs 2 to 2.5 pounds (907.2 to 1,134 g)
- Can move arms and legs freely
- Eyes are now open

End of Eighth Month
- About 16.5 inches (41.25 cm) long
- Weighs about 4 pounds (1.8 kg)
- Hair grows
- Skin gets smoother as a layer of fat develops under it

End of Ninth Month
- 18 to 20 inches (46 to 50 cm) long
- Weighs 7 to 9 pounds (3.2 to 4.1 kg)
- Organs have developed enough to function on their own

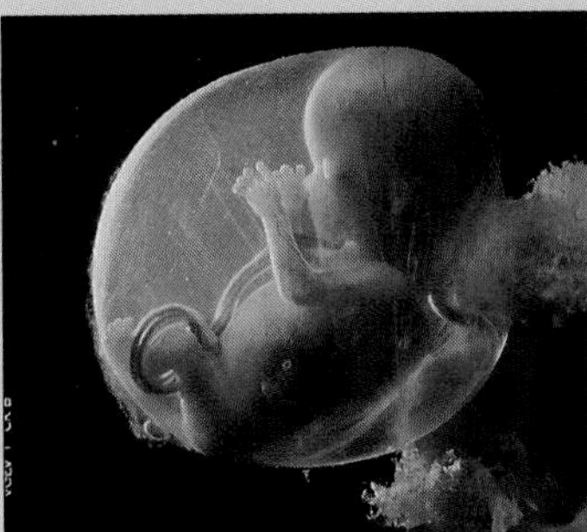

c.

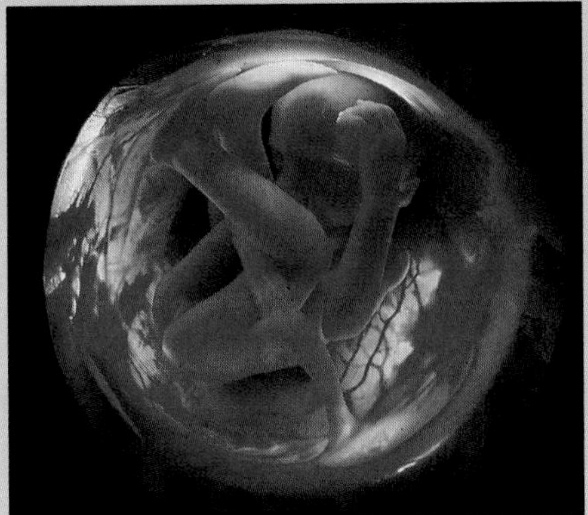

d.

Ultrasound shows information about the fetus.

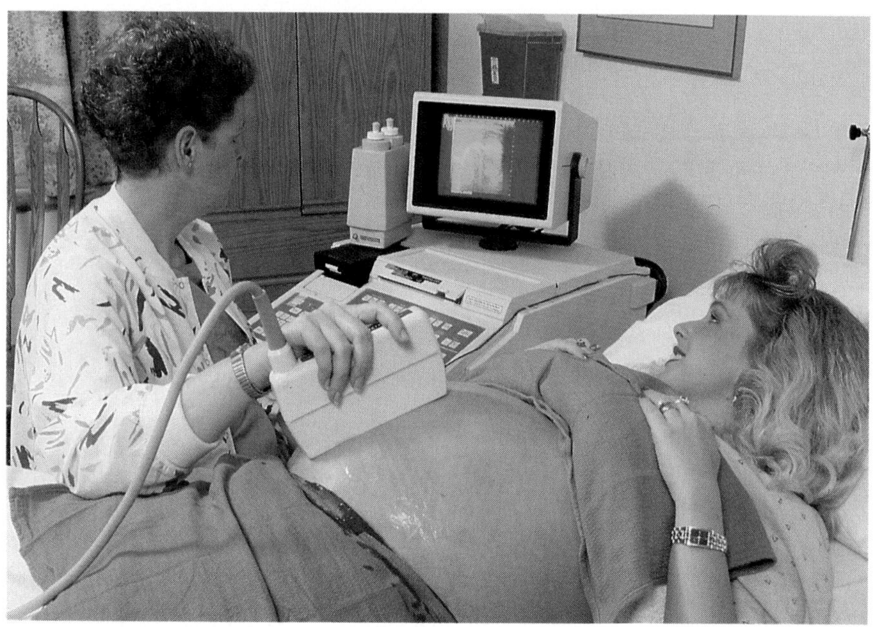

Tests During Pregnancy

A doctor may want to perform tests on a pregnant female to see if the baby is at risk. Sometimes treatment can be done before the baby is born if a problem is detected.

Ultrasound

Ultrasound is a test that uses intermittent high-frequency sound waves to make pictures of the body's inner organs by recording their echoes. This test can be done early in a pregnancy and can be performed several times throughout the pregnancy. An instrument called a transducer is moved back and forth across the abdomen. A computer translates the echoes into pictures on a video screen, making the fetus visible. Ultrasound can be used to check the baby's position as well as the position of the placenta. It can help confirm the date of conception. Ultrasound gives information as to the general development of the fetus.

Amniocentesis

Amniocentesis is a procedure used to reveal chromosomal abnormalities and certain metabolic disorders in the fetus. The test is done after the 16th week of pregnancy. Prior to amniocentesis, ultrasound is used to determine the position of the fetus. Immediately after the ultrasound, the doctor inserts a long thin needle through the abdominal wall and into the uterus. About 4 teaspoons of amniotic fluid are withdrawn. The baby's cells are put in a culture (a prepared solution) where they continue to grow. After two to three weeks, doctors can analyze the chromosomes in the cells for content and number. In addition to identifying chromosomal disorders, the sex of the baby can also be determined since the X or Y chromosome can be seen. Other tests are also available to check the health of the baby and to see if prenatal treatment should be given.

Childbirth

By the ninth month of pregnancy, the baby has turned with its head down in the uterus. The birth process begins with labor pains. Labor begins when a hormone called oxytocin is released from the pituitary gland and travels through the blood to the muscles of the uterus. The hormone causes the uterus to begin contracting. These contractions shorten the muscles of the uterus and begin to pull the cervix, the neck of the uterus, open.

DID YOU KNOW?

- A breech birth is when the baby enters the vagina buttocks or feet first. The danger in a breech birth is that the umbilical cord—the cord connecting the baby and the placenta—can wrap around the baby's neck and cut off the oxygen supply.

Labor and Delivery

For nine months, the cervix has held tightly shut, keeping the baby inside the uterus. Now it must open to a diameter of about 5 inches (13 cm) to allow the baby to pass through. Dilation, or opening of the cervix, is the first and, usually, the longest stage of the birth process.

First Stage of Labor. With each contraction, the baby's head is pushed toward the cervix. As the baby is pushed, its head moves against the membranes of the amniotic sac. The sac ruptures and about one pint of fluid flows out of the vagina. This is often referred to as the breaking of water. It is a sign that birth is close. Sometimes the doctor must break the water to induce birth. The length of this stage varies. If this is the female's first pregnancy, this stage can last 12 hours or more.

Second Stage of Labor. This stage begins with dilation of the cervix and ends with birth. Strong uterine contractions force the baby's head through the vagina—also referred to as the birth canal. *Crowning* is the

HEALTH UPDATE

LOOKING AT TECHNOLOGY

Surgery Before Birth

Some defects that would interfere with organ development can now be corrected before a baby is born. One of these procedures corrects a diaphragmatic hernia, a hole in the diaphragm that allows the intestines, stomach, spleen, and part of the liver to move into the chest cavity.

When this situation happens, the growth of the baby's lungs is stunted, and the baby is unable to breathe when born. The only hope has been to operate on the baby immediately following birth, but this is successful only 25 percent of the time. Now doctors are able to operate on the baby while it is still in the uterus.

To perform this surgery, a small incision is made in the mother's uterus. The baby's chest is opened and abdominal organs are returned to their proper place. Finally a patch is placed over the hole in the diaphragm. The baby now has a good chance to survive after birth. This surgery has been done on babies only 24 weeks beyond conception and only inches in size.

Bonding, or forming a close, personal relationship with a new baby, can begin immediately after birth.

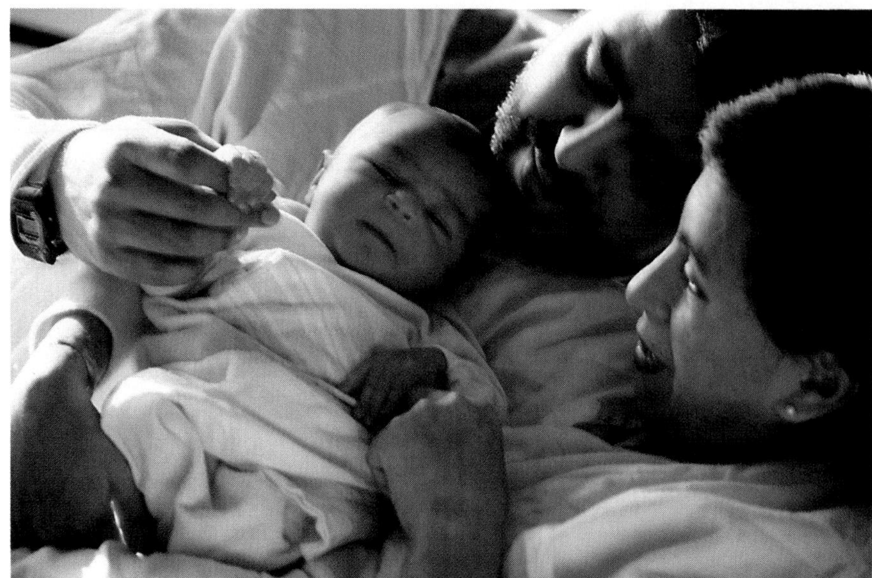

term used to describe when the baby's head can be seen entering the vagina. At this point, the doctor may do an **episiotomy,** which is an incision to open the skin between the vagina and anus to prevent it from tearing. After the baby's head comes out, the body quickly follows. After the birth, the female's tissues are stitched back together. An episiotomy is not necessary for birth, and some females discuss the procedure with their doctor and elect not to have one. Many obstetricians believe it prevents tearing tissue. This stage usually lasts from 1/2 to 1 1/2 hours.

Third Stage of Labor. Uterine contractions continue into the third and final stage of labor. These last about 20 minutes. During this stage, the placenta is fully separated from the endometrium and passes through the vagina. This is called the afterbirth.

DID YOU KNOW?

- Almost all American hospitals administer a routine test to determine an infant's physical condition at birth. This test is named after the late Virginia Apgar, a noted anesthesiologist. The Apgar test measures the baby's condition in five significant areas: appearance or coloring, pulse, grimace or reflex irritability, activity, and respiration. Any significant differences from the normal response in each of these areas may require further testing and observation.

After Delivery

At birth, progesterone levels in the mother's blood drop. This signals the release of another pituitary secretion—prolactin, which stimulates milk production.

For the first few days after the birth, the female's breasts secrete colostrum, which is a yellowish, low-fat, watery fluid she has been producing since the fifth month of pregnancy. If she breast-feeds, on about the third day after birth more nutritious milk is released. Colostrum and milk contain antibodies. These antibodies protect the nursing infant from infections.

The period of time from the birth of the baby until a female begins her menstrual period again is called the **postpartum period.** Her body adjusts to all the changes it has been through and begins to return to its prepregnancy state. Because of the extreme changes in hormones during this time, a female may experience a postpartum let-down. This is sometimes referred to as postpartum depression. Some females may never experience it, others may have a difficult time with it. It is important that the female talk with her doctor so she knows what to expect and can get help if she needs it.

Delivery by Cesarean

Cesarean birth is a method of childbirth in which a surgical incision is made through the abdominal wall and uterus. The baby is lifted out through this opening.

There are numerous reasons a female may need to have a cesarean section (c-section). The baby may not be positioned correctly or may fail to descend into the birth canal. The mother's pelvic structure may be such that vaginal delivery would be dangerous or even impossible. The mother may have active herpes lesions, or scars, which seriously affect a baby passing through the vagina.

Whatever the reason, the doctor and the mother must decide what is safest for the mother and the baby. Some females may have to have a c-section with one delivery, yet will have a vaginal delivery with the next baby.

DID YOU KNOW?

- Despite current, available medical technology, nearly 20 countries report lower infant mortality rates than the United States. In other countries, lower mortality rates are due in part to higher rates of prenatal care. Low birth weight causes infant death. Improper nutrition, smoking, drinking, and illegal drug use cause low birth weight. Infant mortality rates are highest for unmarried mothers.

Childbirth: Options and Trends

Over the years, there have been many changes in the procedures for labor and delivery. Today, a female has many choices, and the father can play a major role in the entire delivery process. The mother and father may choose to attend childbirth classes. Here, they learn to control the mother's breathing and help her relax between contractions. The father can assume the role of coach, helping the mother with the delivery. Many females are choosing natural childbirth rather than taking pain-killing medicines.

Birthing centers are home-like settings available in some hospitals. There, the female can have her baby with her family present if she wishes. Medical facilities are available close by if she should need them. Family members that are going to be present may go through classes to prepare them for the delivery. After the birth, the mother and father may spend as much time with the baby as they wish.

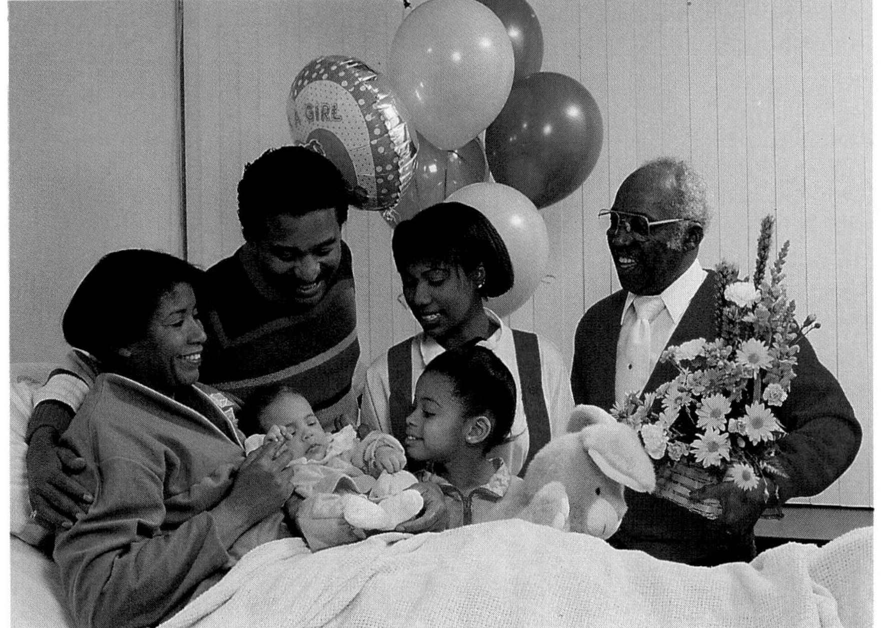

In a birthing center, the new parents and relatives spend as much time as they wish with the new baby.

Some hospitals have a rooming-in arrangement. After delivery, the mother and baby are cared for in the same room. This allows parents to begin developing a bond with their baby immediately. It also gives fathers an opportunity to have a role in child care from the beginning. In traditional hospitals, the baby is taken care of in the nursery.

Problems with Pregnancy

There are more than 2,000 known types of genetic conditions and birth defects. A genetic condition, in the broadest definition, is any quality an individual inherits. However, the term *genetic condition* used in this lesson refers to genetic diseases and disorders, illness, or other conditions of malfunction with which an individual is born.

Birth defects include defects present at birth, including genetic conditions or problems caused by environmental factors. While a majority of birth defects are genetically related, some are the result of environmental factors. This includes disabilities that can occur when the mother has taken certain drugs or has become infected with rubella (German measles) during pregnancy. Some defects are immediately observable at birth. These include physical malformations, such as cleft lip, cleft palate, and clubfoot. While others may be present at birth, testing is required to confirm their presence.

Some conditions that may be present at birth do not generate observable symptoms until the infant is several months to a year or more old. Among these are Tay-Sachs disease (a disorder causing the destruction of the nervous system), cystic fibrosis (a disorder that affects the mucous-secreting glands and the sweat glands), sickle-cell anemia (an inherited blood disorder), phenylketonuria (PKU) (an inherited enzyme deficiency), and hearing loss. Various types of mental retardation, cerebral palsy, and minimal brain dysfunction cannot be observed until the infant begins, or fails to begin, growing through the normal stages of development.

LESSON 2 REVIEW

Reviewing Facts and Vocabulary

1. What is one of the first organs to develop in the embryo?
2. When does an embryo become a fetus?
3. When can the heartbeat of the fetus first be heard?
4. Name two tests that can be done during pregnancy to see if the baby is at risk.

Thinking Critically

5. **Evaluation.** What do you think are the benefits of allowing the father to participate in the birthing process?
6. **Synthesis.** What might be some of the negative consequences of genetic testing?

Applying Health Knowledge

7. Interview a couple who has gone through a cesarean delivery. Find out the reasons for this type of delivery, the outcomes of the delivery, and how the recovery went. Compare these findings with those of a couple who experienced a vaginal delivery.

CHAPTER 6

REVIEW

Reviewing Facts and Vocabulary

1. Why might a female choose to deliver her baby in a birthing center?
2. There are about how many known genetic conditions and birth defects?
3. Describe the third stage of labor.
4. Is the following statement true or false? A couple can assume that their baby is healthy and has no birth defects if the baby is healthy at the time of birth.
5. Give one reason a pregnant female would have an ultrasound.
6. Why might a doctor do an amniocentesis?
7. What is an ectopic pregnancy?
8. When can the developing fetus usually begin to hear sounds?
9. How much does the average baby weigh at birth?
10. Is it possible for a caucasian person to have sickle-cell anemia?
11. Tay-Sachs disease is most common in what group of people?
12. How can smoking cigarettes affect a developing baby?

Thinking Critically

13. **Evaluation.** If you were going to become a parent, would you like to know the sex of your child before delivery? Why or why not?
14. **Evaluation.** Do you think couples should have the right to abort their baby if they find out, through genetic testing, that the child will have serious birth defects? Why or why not?
15. **Synthesis.** What difficulties might a baby with fetal alcohol syndrome have immediately after delivery, and what problems might this child have for the rest of his or her life?
16. **Evaluation.** It has recently been discovered that Parkinson's disease can be controlled and maybe even treated by using the fetal tissue of aborted babies. Considering the benefits to the patients with Parkinson's disease, which are usually elderly patients, do you think this practice could pose a threat to some developing babies?
17. **Analysis.** Compare the accuracy of home pregnancy tests to those tests used to determine pregnancy in doctor's offices. What are a female's best alternatives to knowing for certain that she is or is not pregnant?

Applying Health Knowledge

18. Review the information presented in this chapter. Talk with a couple who is having a child or who have just decided that they would like to have a child soon. Tell them the things you have learned about the pregnancy and birth process.

Beyond the Classroom

19. **Further Study.** Interview a female who has experienced postpartum depression. If you cannot find someone to interview, research the symptoms of postpartum depression at the library. Suggest ways that you think this problem might be treated.
20. **Parental Involvement.** Have your parents tell you about your birth experience. After you have all the information, write a story about your birth. You may want to put your story in book form, including photographs of your mother when she was pregnant with you, other photographs of you soon after birth, or you can draw your own illustrations. Share your story with the class.

CHAPTER

7

Common Concerns of Adolescents

Choosing Abstinence Before Marriage

There is only one method that is 100 percent effective in preventing pregnancy. That is **abstinence,** deciding not to have sexual intercourse. Abstinence does not mean going without a close, special friendship. It also does not mean avoiding all physical contact. Abstinence means not having sexual intercourse. It is important to know that physical or intimate contact between two people can occur without ending in sexual intercourse.

Making a personal decision not to have sexual intercourse is a sign of a mature person who can think independently. However, it is not an easy decision, and it is often not a one-time-only decision. Each time a person is faced with this decision, a choice is made. Someone who has had sexual intercourse before may decide differently the next time. Just because a person has had sex does not mean that he or she will continue with that same decision.

Did you know that almost 50 percent of all high school students have chosen not to have intercourse? Many other teens have had sexual intercourse just one time and then choose abstinence until they are older. These facts may surprise you because we usually hear only about those that do have sex. We do not hear much from or about those who choose to wait.

LESSON 1 FOCUS

Terms to Use

- Abstinence
- Withdrawal

Concepts to Learn

- There are many reasons to wait to have sexual intercourse.
- Withdrawal is not a method to prevent pregnancy.

Deciding to Wait

What are some reasons for deciding to wait to have sexual intercourse?

- A relationship that does not include intercourse can allow the couple to develop a deeper friendship—to establish an intimacy other than sexual intimacy.
- Not having sex offers a couple a chance to explore many different ways to express love and feelings.
- Practicing abstinence reduces both persons' risk of contracting a sexually transmitted disease, including the virus known to cause AIDS.
- Early onset of sexual activity as well as having many sexual partners are risk factors of precancerous lesions and cervical cancer. Abstinence reduces these risks.

As you work on the basic adolescent developmental tasks, consider that abstinence can be a sign of ongoing emotional maturity and responsible behavior. Many young people, males and females, feel pressured into having intercourse before they are ready. It takes an honest, mature person to resist this pressure and make a decision consistent with personal values and goals.

Facts About Pregnancy Prevention

Each year over 1.1 million teenagers become pregnant. The great majority of these pregnancies are unplanned. Lack of correct information, believing wrong information, embarrassment, confusion, and peer pressure are all reasons for this serious problem—a problem that could be prevented.

The most important point to remember in this chapter is that pregnancy occurs when a sperm meets an ovum. Any time sperm are left in or near the opening of the vagina and there is an ovum in a Fallopian tube, there is a chance of pregnancy.

It is very unlikely that an adolescent would know when an ovum is present in a Fallopian tube. Since the adolescent body is going through many changes, it is difficult to determine when an ovum might be there. This means that a female cannot simply count a certain number of days into her cycle and figure out a safe time. During adolescence there is no safe time not to get pregnant. Below are some important facts about pregnancy and pregnancy prevention.

- A female can get pregnant before she starts to menstruate. Once a female begins to ovulate, she can get pregnant. If she gets pregnant after her first ovulation, she would not have had a menstrual period yet.

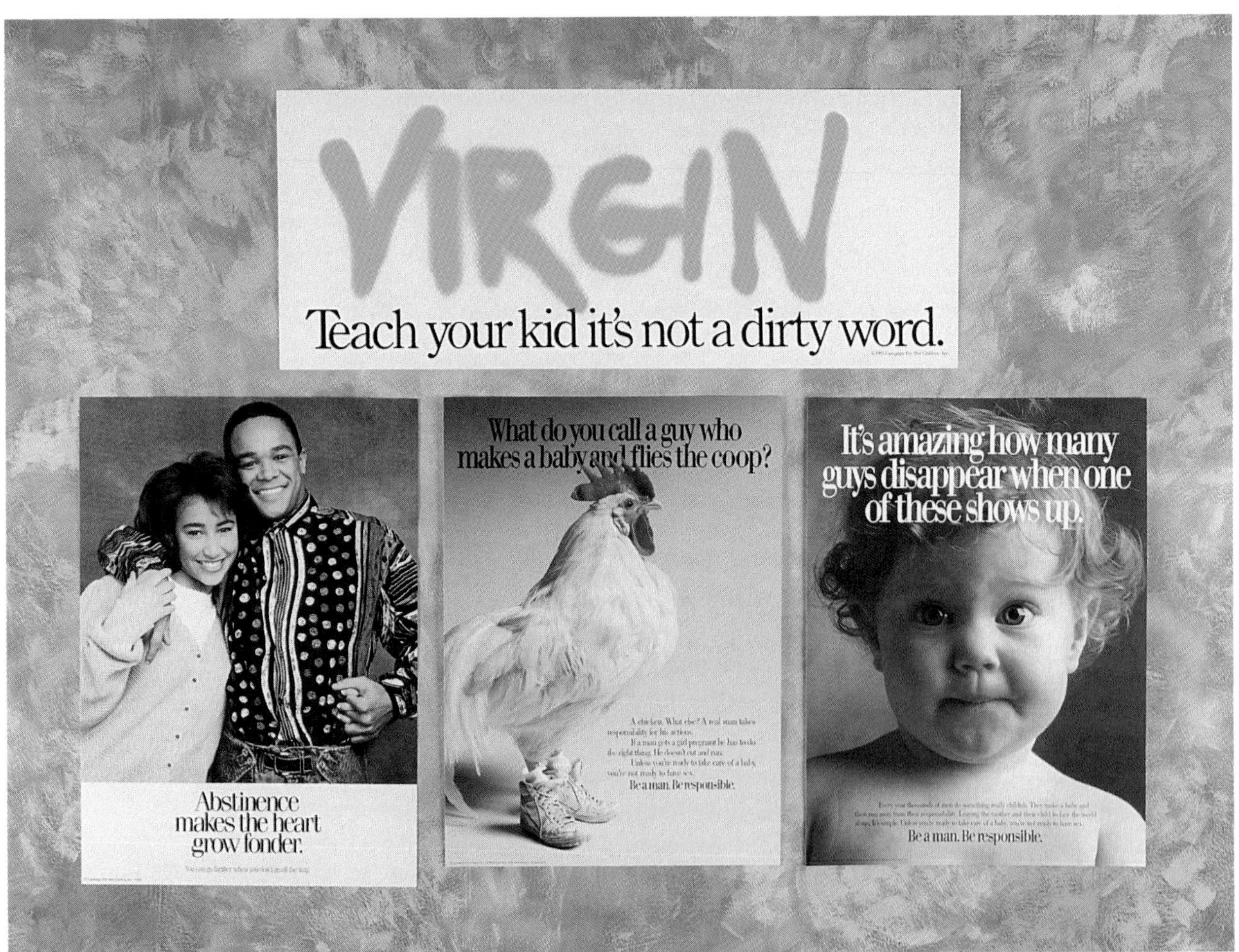

Ads are being used to promote abstinence.

- A female can get pregnant if she has intercourse during her menstrual period. Sperm can live five to seven days in the female's body.
- A female can get pregnant the first time she has intercourse.
- A female cannot flush sperm out by urinating after intercourse.
- Pregnancy can occur even if the couple has sexual intercourse standing up, in a hot tub, or just for a few minutes.
- Douching after intercourse will not prevent pregnancy.
- Withdrawal is not a method of preventing pregnancy. **Withdrawal** means the male removes the penis from the vagina before releasing semen.

Many people may think withdrawal is a method to prevent pregnancy. It is not a reliable method. First, a clear drop of fluid is released from the penis before the semen is released. The fluid, pre-ejaculate, contains sperm. The male has no warning when this fluid is being released. Sperm are left in the vagina, even if he does pull the penis out before ejaculating.

Second, if he does remove the penis before ejaculating and semen is left on the outside of the vagina, there is enough moisture for the sperm to swim into the vagina. Remember, there are 300 to 400 million sperm released with each ejaculation.

Third, withdrawal depends on the male removing the penis at the height of sexual pleasure. He must remain in control. This can be frustrating, and it is easy, as tension increases, to say or think that just this one time nothing will happen. Remember the progression of sexual feelings. As these feelings build, a person tends to think less clearly and may act less responsibly. Not withdrawing his penis just this one time may mean enjoying a few seconds more pleasure and being faced with becoming a parent in nine months. Withdrawal is not a method to prevent pregnancy.

LESSON 1 REVIEW

Reviewing Facts and Vocabulary

1. Define *abstinence,* and discuss its effectiveness in preventing pregnancy.
2. What percentage of high school students have decided not to have intercourse?
3. Name three reasons for deciding not to have intercourse.

Thinking Critically

4. **Synthesis.** How can the progression of sexual feelings diminish the effectiveness of the male using withdrawal to prevent pregnancy during intercourse?
5. **Evaluation.** What would you think if a friend told you that he had not made a decision about whether he will have intercourse. He said he will wait and make his decision when he is out on a date and the situation comes up. Discuss your response.

Applying Health Knowledge

6. Make a list of at least five common myths about pregnancy prevention that you may have heard from your peers. Research and explain why these myths are not true.

CONTRACEPTION

LESSON 2 FOCUS

TERMS TO USE

- Contraception
- Condom
- Spermicide
- Natural family planning (NFP)
- Oral contraceptives
- Diaphragm
- Sterilization

CONCEPTS TO LEARN

- There are many nonprescription methods of birth control.
- After a medical examination, a doctor can prescribe an effective prescription birth control method.

Contra means "against." Conception refers to fertilization and the beginning of pregnancy. **Contraception** means preventing pregnancy. Methods of contraception, or birth control, can be divided into two categories: nonprescription—those that can be purchased in grocery stores or pharmacies; and prescription—those requiring a visit to a clinic or doctor. No form of contraception is 100 percent effective.

Nonprescription Birth Control Methods

Nonprescription methods of birth control include

- a condom,
- contraceptive foam, jelly, suppositories,
- Natural Family Planning (NFP).

The Condom

The **condom** is a thin sheath of latex or animal tissue that is placed on the erect penis to catch semen. The condom acts as a barrier, preventing sperm from entering the vagina.

The condom can be put on the penis only when it is erect. To be effective, it must be put on before there is any contact with the vagina. The condom is unrolled onto the erect penis. A space must be left between the end of the penis and the end of the condom. This space allows room for the semen when it is ejaculated. Without the space, the semen has nowhere to go and is likely to cause the condom to break. Some condoms come with a receptacle tip—a built-in space for the semen.

As soon as the male releases semen, he must hold the condom in place at the base of the penis and immediately remove the penis from the vagina. As long as the penis is erect, the condom will not come off. However, after ejaculation the penis goes soft, leaving room for the condom to slip off and for semen to spill out. Any semen that comes into contact with the vagina could result in pregnancy.

After intercourse, the condom is removed and thrown away. It cannot be reused. The penis should be washed thoroughly to eliminate any sperm. A new condom must be used each time intercourse takes place.

Some condoms are lubricated with a spermicide. A **spermicide** is a chemical that kills sperm that come into contact with it. A spermicide is a second line of defense.

Petroleum jelly, hand lotion, or other petroleum-based products should never be used with condoms since these products can destroy the latex. Heat also destroys latex. Condoms should not be left in glove compartments or carried in wallets for long periods of time. Condoms should be stored in a cool, dry place.

Contraceptive Foam

Contraceptive foam has a spermicide in it. The foam comes in a pressurized can. After shaking the can, an applicator is placed on the top of the can. The pressure causes the foam to fill the applicator. The applicator is then placed in the vagina and the foam is left up close to the cervix.

Foam should be put into the vagina no more than 30 minutes before intercourse. The foam acts as a physical and chemical barrier to the sperm. If foam is inserted and more than 30 minutes pass, another application of foam must be used. It is also recommended that a female not walk or move around a great deal after inserting the foam. A female should never douche after intercourse when using foam.

Contraceptive Jelly

Contraceptive jelly is another type of spermicide. It is used in the same way as foam. It comes in a tube. An applicator is placed on the end of the tube, and the tube is squeezed into the vagina, leaving the jelly close to the cervix. Again, this must be done no more than 30 minutes before intercourse.

Contraceptive Suppositories

Contraceptive suppositories are tabletlike objects that are placed in the upper vagina. Once in the vagina, they dissolve and fill the vagina with a spermicide substance. About 10 to 15 minutes must pass between

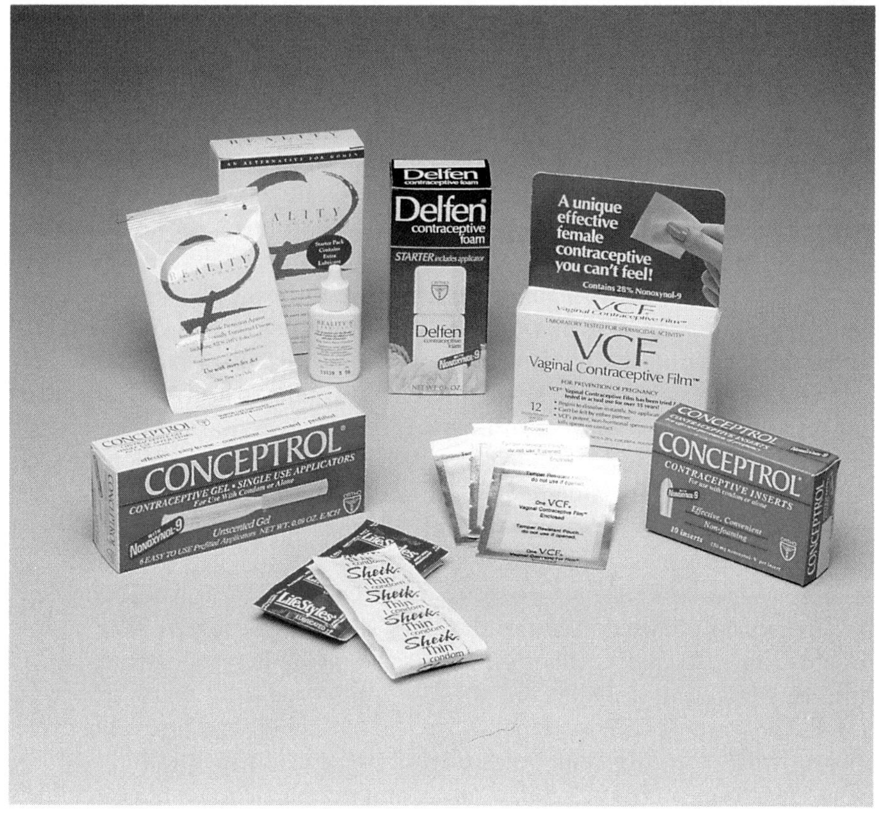

This photo shows kinds of nonprescription birth control methods: Condoms, contraceptive foam, and contraceptive suppositories with applicator.

Seeking the advice and care of a licensed health professional is an important step in maintaining your overall health, sexual and otherwise.

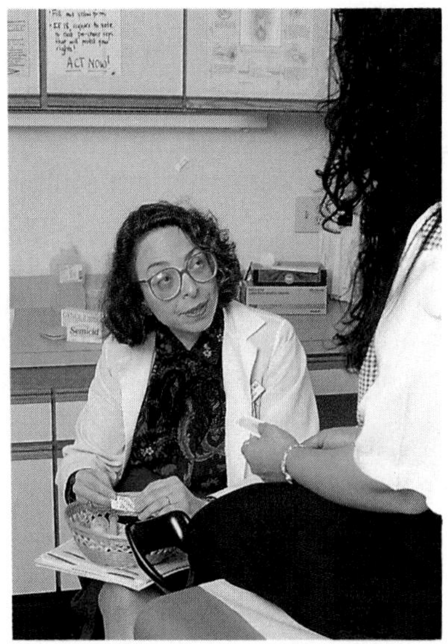

inserting the suppository and having intercourse. This allows time for it to dissolve. As with the foam and jelly, no more than 30 minutes should pass without inserting another tablet. One problem with some suppositories is that the chemicals they contain may cause irritation in the vagina.

When used alone, foams, jellies, and suppositories are certainly better than nothing at all. They are, however, the least effective of the nonprescription methods of contraception. However, when used with the condom, the effectiveness is much higher.

Natural Family Planning (NFP)

Natural family planning (NFP), often referred to as the rhythm method, is a method of contraception that involves determining the fertile days of the female's menstrual cycle. Couples who practice NFP usually attend special classes to learn what is involved in making this method effective. The NFP method of birth control requires careful record-keeping and planning.

A female's body temperature decreases slightly just before ovulation and rises slightly after ovulation. She must take her basal body temperature every morning before getting out of bed. She uses a special thermometer that easily shows slight increases in temperature. She records her temperature daily for several months. At the same time, she checks the mucous secretion from her cervix. She records a description of it on the calendar each day. During ovulation, the mucus changes. It becomes more stringy, less sticky, and clearer in color. Right before ovulation, the amount of mucus increases.

After following these procedures for several months, she can see a pattern and perhaps determine the days she is most fertile. The couple must abstain from intercourse from the end of her menstrual period until three days after ovulation.

This method, of course, depends on the female having a regular cycle. If she ovulates at different times during her cycle, this method will not work. It is especially ineffective for young people. The teenage female's menstrual cycle is usually irregular. Because of the many changes taking place in her body, it is very difficult, if not impossible, to know for sure when she ovulates each month. There is no safe time of the month for a teenage female.

Prescription Birth Control Methods

Prescription methods of birth control are

- oral contraceptives (birth control pills),
- a diaphragm,
- a contraceptive implant.

The Birth Control Pill

Birth control pills are also called **oral contraceptives** since they are taken orally. A birth control pill contains hormones that work the same way as the natural female hormones—estrogen and progesterone. When the pill is taken correctly, these hormones make changes in the female's body that prevent pregnancy. The ovaries stop releasing ova, the mucus from the cervix thickens, and the lining of the uterus changes.

In order to get a prescription for these pills, the female must first visit a health professional. She will be given a pelvic examination that includes a Pap smear. Her blood pressure will be taken. If the doctor feels she can take the pill safely, she will be given a prescription and complete instructions for taking the pill.

The pill must be taken every day to be effective. Protection does not begin until she has taken a full month's cycle. This means that the first month she is on the pill she and her partner must use another method of birth control.

What happens if she misses a pill? If she misses one day, she should take two pills the next day. If she misses more than one day, she should take two pills a day until she is caught up. Missing more than one pill could result in pregnancy. She should continue taking the pills until the packet is empty. For days between packets of pills, the couple must use some other method of birth control for the rest of that cycle.

This photo shows kinds of prescription birth control methods: birth control pills, contraceptive implant, and diaphragm.

Side Effects of the Pill. Much has been written about the pill and its side effects. Side effects are very individual. This is why it is important for the female to have regular checkups with her doctor. If any problem or unusual change takes place, she should notify her doctor.

When a female starts taking the pill, she may notice some physical changes, such as nausea; breast tenderness; breakthrough bleeding or spotting; increased vaginal discharge or mucus; slight weight gain or loss; depression; irritability; or mood changes. These side effects are usually not serious or life-threatening. However, if side effects are very uncomfortable or do not disappear after two or three months, the person should call her doctor or clinic.

A few females develop health problems that are serious while they are taking the pill. These include high blood pressure, blood clots in the veins, or stroke. The pill is not recommended for females with certain health conditions, including migraine headaches, diabetes, and high blood pressure. Females who smoke, who are severely overweight, or

DID YOU KNOW?

- Douching has been used as a process of rinsing out the vagina. It is not a way of preventing pregnancy. Once sperm are left in or near the opening of the vagina, they cannot be rinsed out. Furthermore, the liquid squirted into the vagina will push the sperm upward to the uterus.
- Many doctors suggest that females not douche at all. The body cleanses itself. Douching can change the body's natural environment and leave a female open to infection.

who are 35 years or older have a higher risk of experiencing serious side effects from the pill.

Studies have shown that there is a very low health risk associated with taking birth control pills for most females. The risk is lower than the health risks associated with pregnancy and childbirth.

The pill also has some health benefits. It provides females with some protection against ovarian and uterine cancer, and it reduces the risk of pelvic inflammatory disease, which is a painful infection of the Fallopian tubes, ovaries, or both. The pill also is used to treat endometriosis.

The Diaphragm

The **diaphragm** is a soft rubber cup with a flexible rim that is worn inside the vagina. The cup, or bowl part of the diaphragm, covers the cervix. A special spermicide is applied to the cup. This way, sperm are blocked from entering the uterus and are killed by the spermicidal cream or jelly. The diaphragm is called a barrier method of contraception because it is a physical barrier between sperm and an ovum and pregnancy is usually prevented.

A diaphragm is easy to use and generally comfortable to wear. Usually during intercourse neither the male nor the female can feel it. Diaphragms come in different sizes and styles. A female needs to have a pelvic examination so that the doctor can measure her and give her a correct size diaphragm for her body. She also has to be given instructions for insertion and removal of the device, and an opportunity to practice placing and removing it under the supervision of the nurse or doctor.

As with other methods of birth control, the diaphragm must be used correctly every time intercourse takes place. The diaphragm can be put in up to six hours before intercourse. It must be left in at least six hours after intercourse.

Before inserting the diaphragm, it must be covered with contraceptive jelly. Petroleum jelly is not to be used because it weakens the rubber. If intercourse is repeated, another application of contraceptive jelly must be placed in the vagina, but the diaphragm is not to be removed.

Six hours after the last intercourse, the diaphragm may be removed. Using a finger, the female gets hold of the rim of the diaphragm and slides it out. The diaphragm is then washed with soap and water, rinsed, and patted dry. It is stored in its plastic container. Before putting it away, it should be checked for holes by holding it up to a light and examining its surface carefully. A diaphragm with even a tiny hole or tear is not an effective birth control method. One like that must be replaced immediately. The diaphragm must be refitted if the female gains or loses more than ten pounds, has a baby, or loses a baby before birth.

The Contraceptive Implant

The contraceptive implant involves the insertion of six small matchlike rods under the skin of a female's upper arm. It has only been available since December 1990, when it received approval from the U.S. Food and Drug Administration (FDA). This device is cheaper and more reliable than the pill and, unlike sterilization, can be reversed at any time. The operation, carried out under local anesthetic, begins with the surgeon's making a small puncture in the flesh between the female's elbow and armpit. The device releases small doses of hormones, preventing the release of an ovum from the ovary. It provides protection for a period of five years.

Sterilization

Sterilization is a surgical procedure that makes a male or female incapable of reproducing.

Vasectomy

A vasectomy is a procedure of sterilization for males. The word *vasectomy* means "to cut the vas deferens." A vasectomy is done under local anesthetic.

During this operation, a small incision is made at the top of the scrotum. Each vas deferens is cut and sealed. The procedure takes about 15 or 20 minutes. The male continues to produce sperm, but they are absorbed in his body since they cannot travel into his reproductive tract. He will still be able to ejaculate since the other glands—prostate, Cowper's, and seminal vesicles—continue to produce their fluid. A vasectomy in no way affects a male's masculinity or his sexual drive. It simply prevents sperm from being released from his body.

Since a large amount of sperm is stored in the seminal vesicle, a man who undergoes this operation must have his semen tested about six weeks after surgery. Under a microscope, the doctor can determine if there are any sperm left in his ejaculate. Between the time of the vasectomy and this six-week examination, some other method of birth control must be used. A vasectomy should be considered permanent. However, using microsurgery, the procedure may be reversed. Conception rates may be low after the reversal surgery.

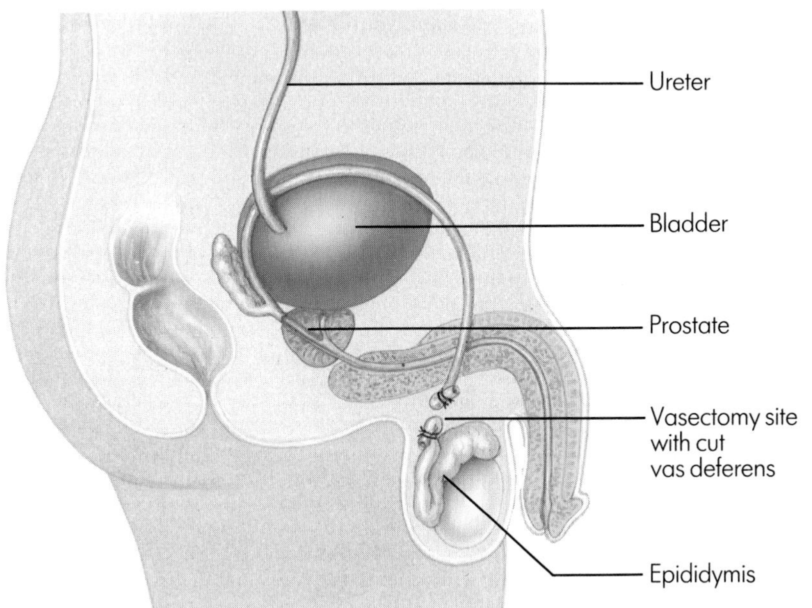

During a vasectomy, each vas deferens is cut and sealed.

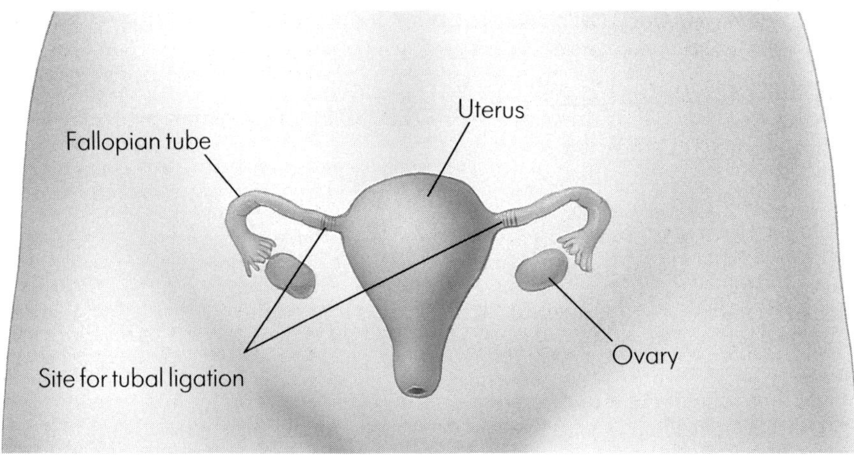

During tubal ligation, the Fallopian tubes are cut and tied off.

Tubal Ligation

In the female, sterilization involves cutting and tying off the Fallopian tubes. This procedure is called a tubal ligation and is often referred to as having the tubes tied.

This operation can be done under local or general anesthesia. Usually a tiny incision is made below the navel. The Fallopian tubes are cut and closed to prevent the sperm and egg from meeting. The tubes may be clamped off or electrically sealed. The ovaries continue releasing eggs, but they disintegrate and are absorbed by the body. The female will continue to have a menstrual period since there is no fertilization. This procedure should be considered permanent. However, there is a small chance of reversal with microsurgery. After this surgery there is limited success of restoring fertility.

LESSON 2 REVIEW

Reviewing Facts and Vocabulary

1. Name three nonprescription methods of birth control.
2. Explain the proper way to use a condom.
3. List five possible side effects of the birth control pill.
4. Define *sterilization,* and give one example of sterilization for males and one for females.

Thinking Critically

5. **Synthesis.** Whose responsibility is birth control—the male's, the female's, or both? Give reasons to support your answer.
6. **Analysis.** Compare the possible effectiveness of the birth control pill to the contraceptive implant.
7. **Evaluation.** Which form of birth control do you think would be most effective for a young married female? Explain your answer.

Applying Health Knowledge

8. Make a chart of each type of birth control method discussed in this lesson. List the name, description, and procedure for using each.

Other Concerns of Adolescents

As you know, there is controversy about some topics related to sexuality. Because some people may feel uncomfortable talking about these topics or find them inappropriate to discuss, there may be a great deal of misinformation passed on about these topics. Unfortunately, the unwillingness to talk about these topics combined with lack of information can cause unnecessary concern and confusion in teenagers. This lesson discusses information about masturbation, homosexuality, and abortion.

LESSON 3 FOCUS

Terms to Use
- Masturbation
- Homosexuality
- Abortion

Concepts to Learn
- People masturbate to relieve sexual tension.
- There are many myths about homosexuality.
- Induced abortion is very controversial.

Masturbation

Masturbation means touching one's own genitals for sexual pleasure. People disagree about whether masturbation is a natural part of growth and development or whether it is wrong and unhealthy. For years, some adults, believing masturbation was wrong and harmful, warned young people of the consequences of such activity. These myths included claims that masturbation caused blindness, insanity, acne, or hair to grow on the palms of the hands. Of course, we know today these claims are not true.

People masturbate to relieve sexual tension. Some people use masturbation as an alternative to sexual intercourse—especially if they do not want to risk a pregnancy or contract an STD, including the virus that causes AIDS. Masturbation does not make a person physically weak, nor does it decrease athletic ability.

Some people choose not to masturbate. This practice may be contrary to their principles or values. It may be something that they are not comfortable with for a variety of reasons.

Masturbation is a private activity that should not affect a person's social growth or ability to make friends. However, any behavior that becomes obsessive (extremely habitual) or interferes with the other areas of a person's life becomes a problem. If people feel guilty about what they are doing, they may experience some psychological stress. If masturbation becomes a problem, it can be helpful to talk with an adult about this concern.

Homosexuality

One of the most emotional issues that relates to sexuality is homosexuality. **Homosexuality** is the state of being homosexual, or having a sexual preference for someone of the same sex. People have very different and strong views on this subject. Unfortunately, many people have very little information or choose to believe wrong information about

One myth about homosexuality is that a person is homosexual because his or her closest friend is of the same sex.

homosexuals. Lack of information often leads to fear. Fear promotes the emotional response people have toward this topic.

There are many myths about homosexuality. One myth is that a person is homosexual because he or she is not yet interested in the opposite sex. This is not true. Everyone's timeline for interest in the opposite sex is different. A person may develop an interest in the opposite sex much earlier or much later than some of his or her friends. Another myth is that a person is homosexual just because his or her closest friend is of the same sex. This myth is false. It is not only normal but healthy to have close, caring friendships with peers of the same sex. Another common myth about homosexuality is that someone who has not had sex—especially if the person is a male—is gay. This is untrue. Having sex or not having sex has nothing to do with sexual preference. Another myth is that you can tell homosexuals by their appearance and mannerisms. Again this is wrong. People should not be judged by the way they look. Incorrect assumptions can be made when people are labeled because of their appearance. Another harmful myth is that homosexuals are child molesters. The vast majority of child molesters are heterosexual males.

Why are some people homosexuals? Researchers have many theories to answer that question. These theories include that a genetic factor is passed to a baby from the parents or that a baby is born with a hormonal imbalance. Another theory is that homosexual behavior is learned from a person's environment.

As research continues, most professionals believe that there may be a combination of factors responsible for homosexuality. Many developmental experts believe that a person's sexual orientation is determined as young as age 5. So debate continues whether or not homosexuality is a matter of choice.

Abortion

An **abortion** is the termination of a pregnancy. A spontaneous abortion, or miscarriage, happens when the uterus contracts and expels its lining. This happens in about 10 percent of all pregnancies. There are a variety of reasons for miscarriage. These reasons include a hormonal deficiency, a faulty ovum or sperm, or a poor endometrium. When miscarriage happens, it is usually early in the pregnancy and is something the female has little or no control over.

An induced abortion takes place in a medical setting with qualified medical professionals to terminate a pregnancy. Under local anesthesia, the doctor breaks down and removes the lining of the uterus and all its contents. This kind of abortion is very controversial. You should discuss with your parents their feelings about this kind of abortion.

Having sex as a teenager can affect many people for a very long time. Often goals and dreams have to be changed. If a teenager chooses to have sexual intercourse, many decisions need to be made. Among these include ways to prevent pregnancy and what to do if the female gets pregnant. However, there is no need to face the problem of an unplanned pregnancy. Pregnancy can be prevented. The safest method of contraception is not to have sexual intercourse. Many young people, both males and females, are choosing abstinence. This is the healthiest choice teenagers can make.

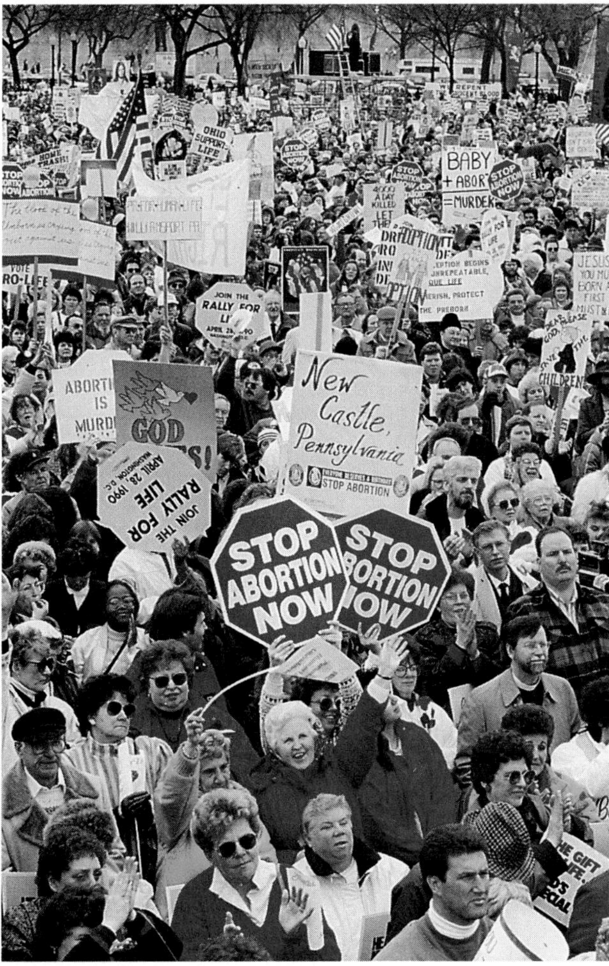

Induced abortion is very controversial. Discuss this topic with your parents.

HEALTH UPDATE

LOOKING AT THE ISSUES

Abortion

On January 22, 1973, the U.S. Supreme Court legalized abortion on demand. However, regulations regarding abortion vary from state to state. Some states allow abortion only if the mother's life is in danger or in cases of rape or incest. Abortion is a very emotional subject. There are two extremely opposed points of view about this topic.

Analyzing Different Viewpoints

ONE VIEW. Many people view abortion as morally wrong and the ultimate child abuse. They state that human life begins at conception, and unborn children should have the same rights as others. They feel abortion kills unborn children, and the law should protect children from this violence. They feel the government should not provide funds for abortions.

A SECOND VIEW. Some groups do not feel a fetus is a person. They distinguish between human life and personhood. They feel birth is the beginning of personhood, defined as the capacity for self-conscious thought and acceptance as a member of society. This side of the abortion issue thinks it is a mother's right to choose whether to give birth or end a pregnancy. They feel the government should provide federal funding for abortions. Many people feel that if abortions are not legalized, females will do it themselves or allow nonmedical persons to do it.

Exploring Your Views

1. What is your view on abortion?
2. Are there certain circumstances when you think abortion might be justified? Explain your answer.
3. How can the number of abortions be reduced?

LESSON 3 REVIEW

Reviewing Facts and Vocabulary

1. Define *homosexuality*.
2. Define the two types of abortion.

Thinking Critically

3. **Synthesis.** Explain possible effects of obsessive masturbation on total health.
4. **Analysis.** Compare the theories presented in this lesson about the origins of homosexuality. Which one are you more likely to agree with? Support your answer.

Applying Health Knowledge

5. Write a paragraph explaining how you might handle a situation in which a friend told you that he or she is a homosexual.
6. Write a letter to an imaginary friend who is choosing to have an abortion. Tell her what your view is on abortion. Include some alternatives that she might consider.

CHAPTER 7

REVIEW

Reviewing Facts and Vocabulary

1. Is the following statement true or false? A female cannot get pregnant if she urinates or douches after having intercourse.
2. Discuss pre-ejaculate and tell whether it can cause pregnancy.
3. Name three prescription forms of birth control.
4. Is it okay to use hand lotion or petroleum jelly instead of spermicide? Explain.
5. Explain how to use contraceptive foam.
6. Define *spontaneous abortion.*
7. For how long does a contraceptive implant provide protection from pregnancy?
8. Explain how a tubal ligation prevents pregnancy.
9. How long should a diaphragm remain in the vagina after intercourse?
10. What is another name for birth control pills?
11. Why is the Natural Family Planning method of birth control ineffective during adolescence?
12. How does the contraceptive sponge prevent pregnancy?
13. What effect does masturbation have on athletic ability?

Thinking Critically

14. **Evaluation.** Do you think the condom is effective in preventing the spread of HIV, the AIDS virus? Why or why not?
15. **Evaluation.** Do you think females under the age of 18 should be required to tell their parents before they get an abortion? Why or why not?
16. **Synthesis.** Name some reasons a male and female might decide on sterilization. How might this affect sexuality?
17. **Synthesis.** If you received conflicting information about birth control from your peers and from your parents, what would you do to find correct information?
18. **Synthesis.** What help could you give to a friend who said she and her boyfriend were having sex but not using any form of birth control?
19. **Analysis.** What is the difference between a physical barrier and chemical methods of contraception? Categorize each method discussed in this chapter. Which one could be considered as both?

Applying Health Knowledge

20. Make a list of the benefits of having sex only in marriage.
21. Why is confidentiality an important aspect of pregnancy testing? Discuss your answers as a group.
22. Your 7-year-old sister asks you what being a homosexual means. She heard kids laughing about this term at school. What would you tell her?

Beyond the Classroom

23. **Community Involvement.** Interview a member of a pro-life and a pro-choice group in your community. Compare their viewpoints. Use the information you gain to add to your opinion on the issue of abortion.
24. **Further Study.** Interview a gynecologist who specializes in fertility. Find out what methods are being used to help infertile couples conceive.
25. **Parental Involvement.** If you were a parent of a 16-year-old, how would you talk with him or her to support the value of abstinence?

CHAPTER

8

SEXUALLY TRANSMITTED DISEASES

Common Sexually Transmitted Diseases

Sexually transmitted diseases (STDs), formerly called venereal diseases (VD), are diseases that spread from person to person through sexual contact. While most common communicable diseases are now being controlled, rates of STDs are still rising. More than 50 STDs are now recognized. About 12 million cases of STDs occur annually. Almost 90 percent occur to those aged 15 through 29. Many of these young people do not even know that they have an STD. Often, there are no symptoms in females. A female could have an STD and be infecting her sexual partner while not even knowing it.

The symptoms of some STDs disappear after a short period of time, so many young people mistakenly think that the disease is gone. But, the disease is still in the body. It may be causing damage to certain body organs, and it may be spread to other people.

Many people do not seek help when they think they have an STD. Most STDs can be completely cured. It can be embarrassing to seek medical help and ask for a test for an STD, so people may ignore symptoms. Of course, such a reaction is dangerous since some STDs cause irreversible damage to the body.

LESSON 1 FOCUS

Terms to Use

- Sexually transmitted diseases (STDs)
- Chlamydia
- Pelvic inflammatory disease (PID)
- Nongonococcal urethritis (NGU)
- Gonorrhea
- Syphilis

Concepts to Learn

- Sexually transmitted diseases are spread from person to person through sexual contact.
- Untreated chlamydia can cause NGU and PID.
- Untreated gonorrhea can lead to sterility in both the male and female.
- Symptoms of syphilis develop in stages.

Who Gets STDs?

Anyone who has sexual contact with another person is at risk of getting an STD. Anyone. Many people have the mistaken idea that only very sexually active people get STDs. This attitude is incorrect. STDs can affect anyone who has sexual intercourse with an infected person.

Unlike some communicable diseases, STDs can be prevented. Choosing not to be sexually active is making a responsible decision. Young people who are not sexually active are not at risk for contracting an STD. Choosing abstinence is a healthy choice.

As with most other topics dealing with sexuality, there is a great deal of misinformation about STDs. This information interferes with preventing STDs. It also keeps people from seeking treatment. As you take more responsibility for your health, it is important that you have accurate information and are able to recognize incorrect information concerning these diseases.

Chlamydia

Most people have heard of gonorrhea, syphilis, and herpes. However, **chlamydia** is the most common STD. There are about four million cases of this infection occurring annually. It is caused by several different microorganisms that are similar to bacteria. Chlamydia attacks the male and female reproductive organs.

FACTS AND MYTHS ABOUT STDS

Take the following quiz about STDs. Determine which statements are facts and which are myths as you read the chapter.

Answer true or false:

1. The body builds an immunity to certain STDs.
2. A person can have more than one STD at the same time.
3. A pregnant female can spread an STD to her unborn child, resulting in birth defects.
4. Once the symptoms of an STD go away, the disease is cured.
5. A person could have an STD and not know it.
6. Complications from an untreated STD can leave a person sterile (unable to have children).
7. A condom is totally effective in preventing the spread of STDs.
8. Having a Pap smear is one way a female can find out if she has an STD.
9. Contraceptive foam or jelly is very effective in preventing the spread of certain STDs.
10. Once a person is cured of an STD, he or she cannot get that particular STD again.

Symptoms

Many people do not realize they have chlamydia until they have serious complications. An estimated 75 percent of females and 15 to 20 percent of males with chlamydia have no symptoms. Symptoms, if they are present, appear within a month after exposure to the infection. If symptoms are present, they may include:

Males

- unusual discharge of fluids from the penis
- painful, burning, or frequent urination

Females

- vaginal discharge of fluids
- pain in the pelvic area
- bleeding between menstrual periods

A pregnant female who has chlamydia can spread it to her baby during delivery. In infants the disease can cause eye infection, blindness, and sometimes pneumonia.

Diagnosis and Treatment

Chlamydia can be hard to diagnose. Many people are infected with chlamydia and gonorrhea at the same time. A laboratory test is used to diagnose the nature of the infection. Antibiotics are the most effective cure.

Dangers of Untreated Chlamydia

If left untreated, chlamydia can cause nongonococcal urethritis (NGU). It can also cause pelvic inflammatory disease. **Pelvic inflammatory disease (PID)** is a painful infection of the Fallopian tubes, ovaries,

DID YOU KNOW?

- PID involves pus that surrounds inflamed tissues, including the Fallopian tubes, the ovaries, or both. This situation can lead to temporary or permanent infertility by partially or totally blocking one or both Fallopian tubes. When one tube is partially blocked, an ovum can be fertilized, but may not be able to pass back through the Fallopian tube to the uterus. An ectopic pregnancy occurs when the ovum implants in the Fallopian tube. As the embryo develops in this type of pregnancy, the Fallopian tube can rupture. Internal bleeding results. This is an emergency situation.

or both. If PID progresses, it can cause scar tissue to develop on the Fallopian tubes. This scar tissue can cause a female to be sterile because the scar tissue blocks the Fallopian tubes. Symptoms may include pelvic pain, chills, fever, irregular menstrual periods, and lower back pain.

In a male, chlamydia can lead to epididymitis, an inflammation of the epididymis. Pain and swelling of the scrotum are signs of this problem. Untreated chlamydia can also cause scarring of the urethra and the vas deferens. Scar tissue on these tubes can leave a male sterile.

Nongonococcal Urethritis (NGU)

Nongonococcal urethritis (NGU) is a disease caused by several different kinds of bacterialike organisms that infect the urethra in males and the cervix in females. Most cases are caused by the chlamydia pathogen. Like all STDs, NGU is transmitted through sexual contact.

Symptoms and Treatment

Males notice symptoms of NGU more than females do. In males, there may be a discharge from the penis anywhere from one to three weeks after infection. Males may also experience a mild burning during urination. Females may have a vaginal discharge and pain in the lower pelvic area.

NGU can be treated and cured. Treatment consists of an antibiotic, usually tetracycline.

Gonorrhea

Next to the common cold and chlamydia, gonorrhea is the most common communicable disease. There are about two million cases of it reported each year. **Gonorrhea** is an STD caused by bacteria that live in warm, moist areas of the body. This bacteria specifically attacks mucous membranes of the penis, vagina, rectum, or throat. The bacteria cannot live outside the body.

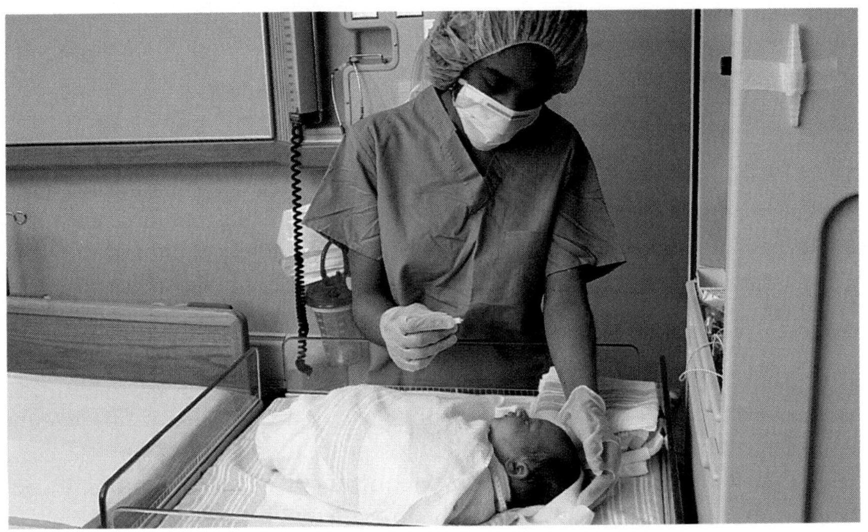

Most states require newborns to be given eye drops to prevent possible infection from gonorrhea, which can lead to blindness.

DID YOU KNOW?

- Unbroken skin is a barrier against pathogens. Therefore you have almost no chance of getting a sexually transmitted disease (including infection from the AIDS virus) from a toilet seat, a public phone, a doorknob, a stairway handrail, or other public items everyone touches.

Symptoms

Symptoms, if they are present, usually appear within three to seven days after sexual contact with an infected person. As with other STDs, however, symptoms are not always obvious. This is particularly true in the female who may never know that she has gonorrhea. Symptoms may not be present or may be so slight that they go unnoticed. If present, symptoms will go away on their own, but the disease still remains in the body.

In a male, symptoms usually include a thick, whitish-yellow discharge from the penis. He may also experience a burning sensation when urinating. Again, a male might have one or both of these symptoms, or he may have no symptoms at all.

A female may have a yellow-green discharge from the vagina, abdominal pain, frequent urination, and a burning sensation when urinating. However, these symptoms can also be caused by other diseases. Gonorrhea can result in PID.

Diagnosis and Treatment

Gonorrhea can only be confirmed by a medical diagnosis. In a male, gonorrhea is diagnosed by examining the discharge from the penis under a microscope. In a female, a culture test of the vagina is done to make the diagnosis. A sample of cells is taken from the vagina and examined under a microscope. The Pap smear, which is a test for cervical cancer, does not test for gonorrhea.

Most cases of gonorrhea can be quickly and easily cured if diagnosis is made early. Antibiotics, such as penicillin or tetracycline, are the usual treatment. There is presently a new strain of gonorrhea that is resistant to penicillin. With this particular strain, a different antibiotic is used. Being cured of gonorrhea does not protect a person from getting the disease again. The body does not build an immunity to any of the STDs.

If gonorrhea is not diagnosed and treated, the disease spreads in the body. It causes serious damage to the body, such as arthritis or heart damage.

Dangers of Untreated Gonorrhea

In both males and females, untreated gonorrhea can lead to sterility—the inability to reproduce. In addition, the male can have epididymitis and damage to the urethra. In the female, PID can occur. This complication can result even if the disease is treated. If not diagnosed or treated, gonorrhea in both males and females can spread to other parts of the body, causing damage to joints, heart tissue, and other organs. In the female, PID can occur.

In pregnant females, gonorrhea increases the chance of premature labor and stillbirth. If a female has gonorrhea when she gives birth, the bacteria that cause the disease can enter the baby's eyes. The baby can develop an eye infection that can lead to permanent blindness. For this reason, most states have a law that requires all newborn babies to be treated with special eye drops shortly after birth.

Syphilis

Syphilis is a disease caused by a bacterium called a spirochete. It is one of the most dangerous sexually transmitted diseases. It enters the body through the soft inner skin, usually in the vagina, anus, penis, or mouth. Once in the body, the bacteria enter the blood and infect the entire body. Syphilis can be life-threatening to males and females, and to any future children a female may have. When left untreated, it can cause heart disease, blindness, paralysis, and insanity.

Symptoms

Symptoms of syphilis develop in stages. They appear and then go away without treatment. The disease, however, continues to progress in the body. Symptoms appear within 10 to 90 days (average is three weeks) after sexual intercourse with an infected person.

Primary Stage. The first stage of syphilis is characterized by a small, red painless sore called a chancre. The chancre usually appears where the pathogen entered the body. In males, chancres are usually on the penis. In females, they are less noticeable since they may appear in the vagina, on the cervix, or in the folds of the labias. The chancre will disappear within one to five weeks. However, the disease continues to develop in the body.

Secondary Stage. Within one to five months after being infected with the syphilis bacteria, the disease usually produces symptoms that include muscular or joint pain, swollen lymph nodes, nausea, headache, loss of appetite, fever, and a general sick feeling. During this stage, body organs may be damaged. The most common symptom during this second stage of syphilis is a highly contagious rash. The rash may appear anywhere on the body. In females, it usually appears on the outer edge of the vagina. The rash develops into sores, which ooze a clear fluid with the infectious spirochetes. These sores provide an easy entry and exit route for the virus that causes AIDS. Without treatment, the second phase of syphilis usually passes in 4 to 12 weeks.

The rash that is caused by syphilis can appear anywhere on the body.

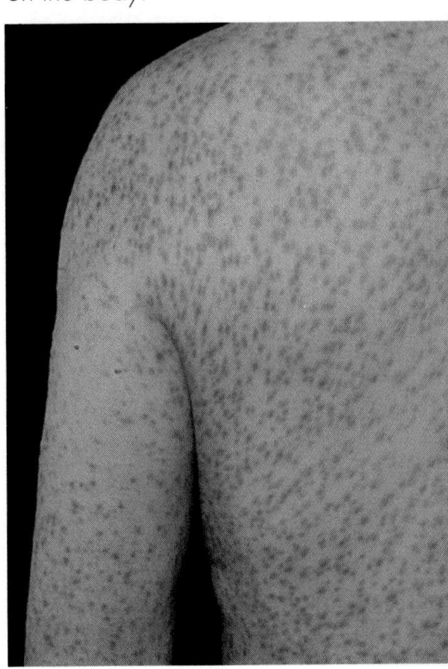

Latent Stage. The third stage begins about two or more years after the initial infection. During this stage, symptoms have disappeared, infected persons often think that they are cured or didn't have the disease after all.

Neurosyphilis Stage. Years after infection, the bacteria begin to attack the heart, blood vessels, bones, liver, and central nervous system. Damage to the tissue of these organs is slow and steady. A person may experience blindness or insanity.

Diagnosis and Treatment

While gonorrhea is detected by means of a microscopic slide exam, the test for syphilis, called the Venereal Disease Research Laboratory, or VDRL, is a blood test. The presence of the spirochete in the blood or from the sores indicates the presence of the disease. Some states demand that couples who plan to marry have a blood test for syphilis before doing so.

Tetracycline or penicillin are the main drugs used in the treatment of syphilis. Doctors strongly recommend follow-up exams to be sure that the disease has been cured. No matter how effective the treatment can be, it can only stop the disease from progressing. It cannot repair any harm that has already been done, so early treatment of syphilis is crucial.

No one has immunity to syphilis. A person may become reinfected at any time. If an individual goes through too many treatments, the body may become immune to penicillin as a means of treatment.

Congenital Syphilis

A pregnant female who has syphilis is likely to transfer the infection to her unborn child. This condition is called congenital syphilis. *Congenital* means "existing at or dating from birth." The unborn child can develop syphilis any time after the fifth month of pregnancy. The mother's chances of having a miscarriage are four times greater if she has syphilis, and her chances of having a stillborn baby are doubled. If the baby is born, symptoms of congenital syphilis begin to appear within three to four weeks. Late congenital syphilis can result in deafness, damage to bone, teeth, and liver, and hydrocephalus. This condition results with cerebral spinal fluid accumulating inside an infant's head. If syphilis is diagnosed early enough in the mother, penicillin treatment will usually protect the unborn fetus.

LESSON 1 REVIEW

Reviewing Facts and Vocabulary

1. Define *sexually transmitted disease,* and tell who can get an STD.
2. What is the most common STD, and what are the symptoms?
3. Name some of the results of untreated gonorrhea.
4. How can an unborn baby get syphilis?

Thinking Critically

5. **Evaluation.** Why do you think people might not go for treatment if they thought they had an STD?
6. **Synthesis.** What advice would you give a friend who had a chancre on the genitals that disappeared within two weeks?

Applying Health Knowledge

7. Write your own STD quiz, similar to the one in Lesson 1. Have your friends and family tell whether the statements are true or false. Find out what myths about STDs are believed most frequently.

LESSON 2

Other Sexually Transmitted Diseases

Other STDs include herpes simplex virus 2, vaginitis, genital warts, pubic lice, and scabies.

Herpes Simplex Virus Type 2

In the past, **herpes simplex virus (HSV)** has been divided into two types—HSV 1, a virus that causes cold sores on the mouth, and HSV 2, a virus that causes genital sores. However, either type can cause herpes sores in the genital area or on any other part of the body. For this reason, medical professionals are no longer distinguishing between herpes 1 and 2. Genital herpes is most often spread through sexual contact. However, transmission can occur when any body surface makes direct contact with a herpes sore. For the purposes of this section, the virus, when transmitted through sexual contact, is described as herpes type 2. This type does have certain characteristics.

Symptoms

With the first outbreak of herpes, blisterlike bumps will usually begin 2 to 20 days after contact with the virus. Enlarged lymph nodes, fever, headaches, and/or fatigue may also be present with the first infection. Some people will experience warning signs of an outbreak before the blisters actually appear. These signs include itching, burning, a feeling of pressure, or increased sensitivity in the infected area. Some females may also experience a vaginal discharge or pain when urinating.

This first infection may last as long as three weeks. Health care is very important when the blisters are present. Anyone with an outbreak of herpes should avoid touching the lesions. Hands should always be washed, especially after using the bathroom. Health care helps prevent spreading the virus to other parts of the body.

Diagnosis and Treatment

A tissue culture is the test used to diagnose herpes 2. Currently, no cure exists for herpes 2, but there is treatment, such as Acyclovir that may suppress it in an individual.

The blisterlike sores of herpes 2 go away, but the virus remains in the body. Blisters may reappear at any time. Also, when the blisters are present, the disease can be transmitted to another person.

However, one of the problems with this virus is that the disease may be contagious for a period of time before the blisters appear and after they go away. There is no sure way of knowing when the disease is in its contagious state. This makes controlling its spread very difficult.

LESSON 2 FOCUS

Terms to Use

- Herpes simplex virus (HSV)
- Vaginitis
- Genital warts
- Pubic lice
- Scabies

Concepts to Learn

- Emotional stress and fatigue can cause outbreaks of the herpes virus.
- There are several types of vaginitis.
- Genital warts are highly contagious.
- Pubic lice attach to hair follicles and deposit their eggs near the base of the hair shaft.

One of the problems in preventing the spread of herpes 2 is that the individual may be contagious even before blisters appear.

Although the symptoms of herpes 2 go away, the virus remains in the body in such a state that it may be reactivated to cause another rash. After the healing from the initial outbreak has taken place, the virus enters nerve endings near the initial rash. The virus moves away from the surface of the skin, thus escaping the body's defenses. It moves to nerve-cell bodies near the spinal cord, where it becomes dormant (inactive). Dormant herpes 2 virus can remain in this state indefinitely without causing damage.

Some people never have another outbreak of the virus, while others experience periodic outbreaks. Different factors, which are very individual, influence recurring outbreaks. It is not known exactly what triggers these outbreaks. Emotional stress, fatigue, excessive exposure to sunlight, menstruation, poor diet, or friction from tight clothing have all been identified as factors that have caused the reactivation of the virus. Infected females should have regular Pap smears, since herpes 2 infections have been linked to the development of cervical cancer cells.

Some people experience a great deal of discomfort when the blisters are present. To aid in healing, these blisters must be kept clean and dry. Loose-fitting clothing and cotton underwear help keep them dry and can reduce the discomfort.

Acyclovir is presently the only approved medication being used for herpes patients. It may be helpful in relieving the pain or making the sores heal faster. It does not prevent further outbreaks of the virus.

Pregnant Females and Herpes 2

Pregnant females who have a herpes 2 infection run a higher risk of miscarriage or premature birth. There is also a high death rate among babies born to mothers who have the herpes 2 infection. Babies have a higher risk of brain damage if they pass through the birth canal at a time when the infection is active. A pregnant female should inform her doctor if she knows or suspects that she has herpes 2. A doctor can perform a caesarean delivery to avoid any risk to the baby.

Vaginitis

Vaginitis is an inflammation of the vagina. It is a very common condition and affects most females at some time. It is most often caused by an infection within the vagina that causes itching or burning around the opening of the vagina. The female may also notice an unusual discharge—different from the normal daily discharge from the vagina. The unusual discharge may also have an unpleasant odor. Any change like this is a sign to a female that something is wrong. She should visit a doctor or a clinic for treatment.

Types of Vaginitis

There are several types of vaginitis. The three most common are yeast, also called moniliasis; nonspecific vaginitis; and trichomoniasis infection.

- Nonspecific vaginitis is caused by bacteria. Symptoms include itching, burning with urination, and an odorless discharge.

HEALTH UPDATE

LOOKING AT THE ISSUES

STD Payment

In the past few years, persons who have been infected with a sexually transmitted disease have sued former partners who gave it to them and have won in court. For example, the Ohio Supreme Court has ruled that a person with a sexually transmitted disease should abstain from sexual intercourse or warn others that he or she is infected before having sexual intercourse.

Analyzing Different Viewpoints

ONE VIEW. This ruling is fair. A person should be held responsible for his or her actions.

A SECOND VIEW. This ruling is unfair. Every person, not just those who are infected, should take responsibility for his or her actions and be aware of all risks involved.

Exploring Your Views

1. What is your opinion about this ruling?
2. If you were a judge, how would you rule in a case like this?
3. Do you think this ruling will deter teens from having sex? Explain.

- Trichomoniasis infection often occurs at the end of the menstrual cycle. It is caused by a protozoan. Symptoms include itching, burning with urination, and a yellowish discharge with an unpleasant odor.
- Yeast infections are caused by a fungus. Symptoms include a thick, white cheesy discharge, genital itching, and irritation.

All of these infections can be passed from one sexual partner to another. Trichomoniasis is most often transmitted in this way. However, a female can develop a yeast infection without having had sexual contact. She can then infect her partner if she does have sexual contact.

Organisms that cause vaginitis can invade the male urethra by the opening through which a male urinates and can go to other organs in the male reproductive system. The male is likely to have no symptoms at all. However, he is contagious and will infect anyone he has sexual contact with.

If a female suspects that she has vaginitis, she should refrain from sexual intercourse. She could infect her partner. Once diagnosed, the doctor may have her ask her partner to be checked. If he has contracted the organisms, he will need to use a prescribed medication also.

Prevention of Vaginitis

Organisms that cause vaginitis thrive in moisture. For this reason, the genital area should be kept as dry as possible. Wearing cotton underwear and panty hose with a cotton crotch allows air to circulate and helps keep this area dry. Not wearing tight pants may also help prevent vaginitis. Keeping the vaginal area clean is important. Wash only with mild soap. Rinse thoroughly after washing and dry completely.

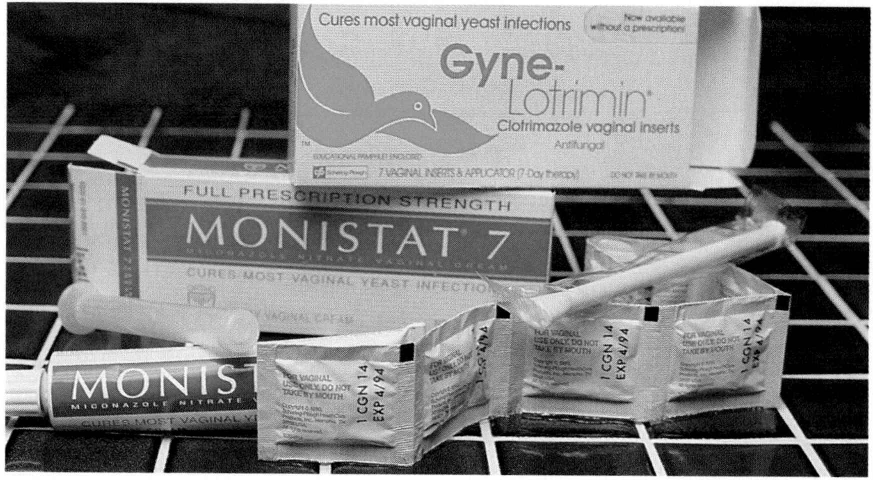

Treatment for some vaginal infections includes over-the-counter medicines.

Good health habits can reduce the risk of getting vaginitis. However, since it is such a common infection, be alert to the symptoms. Contact a doctor or clinic if any such symptoms appear. Proper diagnosis and prompt treatment are important.

Genital Warts

Genital warts, also called venereal warts, are transmitted only sexually and are highly contagious. Genital warts may be caused by a number of different viruses. The viruses that cause genital warts differ from those that cause warts on the hands or feet.

The most common genital warts grow in small, cauliflower-like clusters. They thrive on wet surfaces and between folds of skin. Genital warts are most often found on the genitals and between the buttocks. Warts may also be found under the foreskin on an uncircumcised penis.

Warts have quite a long incubation period—taking as long as six months to appear after exposure. The average incubation period is two to three months. An infected person can pass the virus on before the warts appear. Genital warts must be diagnosed at a clinic or by a doctor. There are several methods of treatment that are successful.

Pubic Lice

Pubic lice are parasites and are also known as crabs. They are crab-like insects that infest pubic hair and feed on human blood. They attach to hair follicles and deposit their eggs near the base of the hair shaft.

The primary symptom of pubic lice is intense itching. Bloodstains may also be noticed on underwear. Symptoms usually appear about 25 to 30 days after exposure.

Crabs are usually spread by intimate physical contact with an infected person. Crabs will die within 24 hours after separation from the human body. However, the eggs can live up to six days. A person could also get crabs by coming into contact with infected bedding, clothing, or towels.

Crabs can be cured by using a special medicated shampoo. Directions must be followed carefully. All of the infected person's clothing, bedding, and other laundry must be washed in hot water with a detergent or dry cleaned.

Special medicated shampoos help eliminate pubic lice.

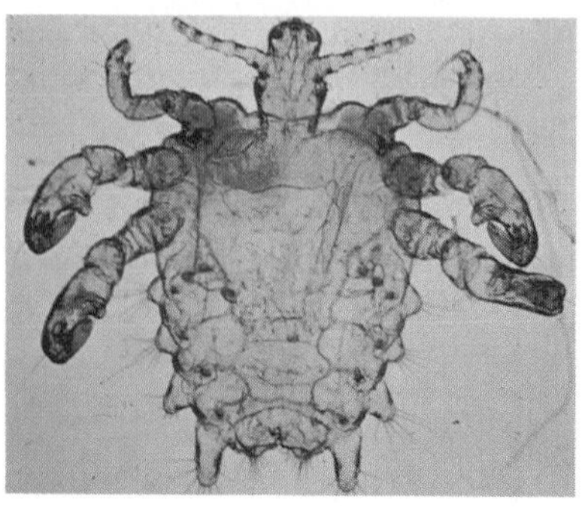

Scabies

Scabies are tiny parasitic mites that burrow in the skin. They are not always acquired by sexual contact. Close bodily contact is a common way to transmit them.

Itching in the genital area occurs four to six weeks after infection. The mites can be spread to other body areas—especially the fingers and forearms—by touching the genital area. Hot baths and medicated creams can cure this problem.

Making Responsible Decisions

STDs can be completely prevented. Prevention is every individual's responsibility. A person who chooses not to have sexual intercourse does not have to worry about getting an STD.

Treatment for all STDs is also an important personal responsibility. Having an STD is not like having a cold. It will not simply go away if a person waits long enough. The individual must do something about it. It is not a time for embarrassment. A person who seeks treatment from a doctor in private practice or a public health clinic is guaranteed by law that all information will remain confidential. However, it is important that the infected person notify everyone with whom he or she has had any sexual contact.

A person who decides to have sexual intercourse must take responsibility for that decision. Getting to know the person he or she is in a relationship with is an important step. The two people should talk about protecting their health and well-being. Using condoms and contraceptive foam may help protect against STDs. Washing with soap and water after intercourse also can provide some protection. However, a responsible decision is your best protection. The most responsible and healthiest choice is not to have sexual intercourse.

LESSON 2 REVIEW

Reviewing Facts and Vocabulary

1. List the symptoms of herpes simplex virus 2.
2. Name the three most common types of vaginitis.
3. How might vaginitis be prevented?

Thinking Critically

4. **Synthesis.** Discuss what a person should do if he or she found out they had genital warts, but had had sexual contact with three different partners within the past nine months.
5. **Evaluation.** Do you think that an individual should be required by law to tell doctors or health clinic personnel who his or her sexual partners are if it is discovered that the person has an STD? Why or why not?

Applying Health Knowledge

6. Write a story about someone who contracts an STD. Include symptoms of the STD and tell what treatment the person must follow. Describe the dangers if the STD is not treated.

CHAPTER 8

Review

Reviewing Facts and Vocabulary

1. What is the most effective way to avoid getting an STD?
2. Can males, females, or both get chlamydia?
3. Tell which of the following statements is true:
   a. A person can always tell if he or she has an STD.
   b. A person cannot get an STD if he or she uses a condom.
   c. A person could have an STD and not know it.
4. Describe the neurosyphilis stage of syphilis.
5. Explain how crabs live on the human body.
6. How long can it take for genital warts to appear?
7. Define scabies and tell how they can be cured.
8. How would a doctor find out whether a person has syphilis?
9. How are newborn babies protected from getting eye infections or blindness caused by gonorrhea?
10. Explain how pelvic inflammatory disease can lead to sterility in females.

Thinking Critically

11. **Evaluation.** What would you think and how would you react if your friend told you that she had crabs?
12. **Synthesis.** In terms of prevention, what advantages do STDs have over most other communicable diseases, such as the common cold?
13. **Evaluation.** Do you think doctors should be required to inform the parents of a patient under the age of 18 who has an STD? Why or why not?
14. **Synthesis.** What might be the consequences if a person infected with an STD never told his or her sexual partners that he or she had an STD?

Applying Health Knowledge

15. In groups of two or three, devise a game to help classmates keep the facts straight about STDs.
16. What type of STD clinics are available in your community?
17. What are some reasons for the continued increase in the rates of STDs? What might be done to help curb the rates?
18. Write a 30-second radio announcement promoting prevention of STDs.
19. What would you tell a class of eighth graders about STDs?
20. Why do you think STDs are such a serious problem in the adolescent age group?

Beyond the Classroom

21. **Parental Involvement.** Invite parents into the classroom to debate the issues of STDs, medical information, and privacy. Discuss whether adolescents, adults, or anyone should be required to inform anyone else of their STD.
22. **Further Study.** Research to find further information about a particular STD. Write a report to share with the class. Include symptoms, diagnosis, treatment, and dangers that can occur when the STD is not treated. Include a visual aid when presenting the report to the class.

CHAPTER

9

AIDS

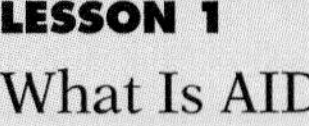

WHAT IS AIDS?

LESSON 1 FOCUS

TERMS TO USE

- Acquired immune deficiency syndrome (AIDS)
- Human immunodeficiency (IM•yuh•noh•di•FISH•uhn•see) virus (HIV)
- Lymphocytes (LIM•fuh•syts)
- Antibodies

CONCEPTS TO LEARN

- AIDS is the final stage of infection caused by the human immunodeficiency virus (HIV).
- To date, HIV is known to be transmitted only through blood, vaginal secretions, semen, and breast milk.
- Specific behaviors are known to transmit HIV from an infected to an uninfected person.
- HIV is not transmitted through casual contact.

Acquired immune deficiency syndrome (AIDS) is a fatal communicable disease with no effective treatment or known cure. AIDS is the final stage of infection caused by the **human immunodeficiency virus (HIV).** When HIV enters the body, it attacks the immune system.

How Does HIV Affect the Body?

In order to understand how HIV attacks the body's immune system, it is necessary to review the function of lymphocytes. HIV causes specific changes in the functions of the lymphocytes, which differ from changes caused by other kinds of viruses.

Lymphocytes and Antibodies

Lymphocytes are white blood cells made in bone marrow. Lymphocytes move throughout your lymphatic system between blood and lymph tissue and help your body fight pathogens, disease-causing organisms. There are two major types of lymphocytes—B cells, which mature in bone marrow, and T cells, which mature in the thymus gland. T helper cells, a type of T cell, stimulate B cells to produce antibodies. **Antibodies** are proteins that help destroy pathogens that enter the body.

When HIV enters the body, it enters certain cells, including T helper cells. Here HIV reproduces its genetic material, which causes more T helper cells to become infected and to be destroyed. This decrease in the number of T helper cells affects the ability of the immune system to fight pathogens. As a result, many illnesses can occur in the body. Indicator illnesses are those illnesses associated with a person who has AIDS. These include opportunistic infections, which are infections a healthy immune system would usually be able to fight. A person is said to have the disease AIDS when he or she is infected with HIV, has a low T helper cell count, and has one or more indicator illnesses.

Origin of HIV

There are many theories as to where HIV originated and how it spread to the United States. It is thought that the virus spread as people traveled. It is also thought that over time the virus has changed in order to survive.

The first group of people in the United States diagnosed with AIDS were male homosexuals. Many people then believed AIDS was a disease only homosexuals could contract. This is not true. Anyone who participates in behaviors known to spread HIV is at risk of becoming infected, regardless of age, race, or sexual orientation.

How HIV Is Transmitted

There are many myths about how HIV is or is not spread. The fact is, HIV must enter a person's blood to infect the person. HIV has been found in body fluids such as blood, semen, and vaginal secretions of infected persons. Small concentrations have also been found in saliva, sweat, tears, feces, urine, and breast milk. To date, HIV is known to be transmitted only through blood, vaginal secretions, semen, and breast milk. Certain behaviors and situations are known to transmit HIV from an infected to an uninfected person. These behaviors and situations transmit the bodily fluids mentioned before.

Behaviors Known to Transmit HIV

About 93 percent of adults and teenagers testing positive for HIV have acquired the virus through sexual intercourse or IV drug use. These two actions are high-risk behaviors for HIV infection.

Sexual Intercourse. HIV can be transmitted during any form of sexual intercourse. During intercourse, secretions containing HIV can enter a partner's blood through tiny cuts in the body. The risks of HIV infection increase with the number of sexual partners a person has or by having sexual contact with someone who has had many sexual partners. Having an STD that results in sores and bleeding or discharge also increases the risks of HIV entering the blood.

Contaminated Needles. If a person who is infected with HIV injects drugs into his or her veins with a syringe, drops of that person's blood are left on the needle. If another person uses the same needle, it is very likely that the infected blood will be passed to this person's blood. Sharing any needle, including one used to inject steroids, to make tattoos, or to pierce ears puts a person at risk of becoming infected with HIV.

Blood that is donated in the United States is tested for the presence of HIV antibodies.

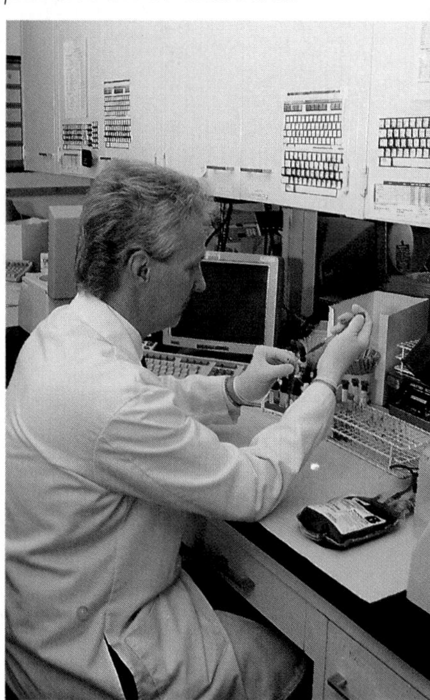

Situations Known to Transmit HIV

HIV is carried in the blood. Any transfer of blood from one person to another is a potential risk for HIV infection.

Blood Transfusion. Prior to March 1985, before donated blood was tested for HIV, people who received blood transfusions were at risk of being exposed to HIV. All blood donated in the United States is now tested for the presence of HIV antibodies. This testing has almost eliminated the risk of receiving contaminated blood or blood products from a transfusion. There is no risk of HIV infection when donating blood because disposable needles are used. These needles are used only one time.

Before, During, and After Birth. A pregnant female who is infected with HIV can pass the virus to the baby in blood exchanged through the umbilical cord. A baby also could receive HIV during birth if HIV enters a cut on the baby's body. A nursing baby could receive HIV while breast-feeding.

HIV is not transmitted through casual contact.

Teenagers at Risk

Teenagers are now a primary risk group for contracting HIV. The Centers for Disease Control and Prevention (CDC) is part of the United States Department of Health and Human Services. The CDC gathers statistics regarding disease throughout the world. According to the CDC:

- The number of AIDS cases in people between the ages of 20–24 as of December 31, 1994, totaled 16,575. Most of these people probably became infected with HIV as teenagers.
- The cases of AIDS among teenagers that had been reported as of December 31, 1994, totaled 1,965.
- AIDS now exceeds accidents as the leading cause of death among young adults.

A teen who chooses to abstain from sexual intercourse and who does not use intravenous (IV) drugs greatly reduces the risk of HIV infection. Abstaining from the use of alcohol and other drugs, which can impair a person's judgment in regard to sexual activity and drug use, can also reduce the risk of HIV infection. Making responsible decisions means protection from HIV infection.

How HIV Is Not Transmitted

Fear of AIDS has caused people to react negatively and sometimes violently toward people known to be infected with HIV. Ignorance feeds this fear. Remember, HIV is transmitted in body fluids. It is not an airborne pathogen.

HIV cannot be transmitted through casual contact. Casual contact includes sharing towels, combs, eating utensils, bathroom facilities, or having close physical contact, such as touching or hugging. In studies of families who have a member infected with HIV, no incidence of the virus spreading to other family members through casual contact has been found. In addition, according to the Centers for Disease Control, HIV is not spread through an insect bite.

DID YOU KNOW?

- Tuberculosis (TB) is a communicable disease caused by a bacterium. TB is spread through the air when particles are coughed up. TB almost always affects the lungs but can attack almost any other body part. The initial effect of TB results in damage to and death of the infected areas. As the disease progresses, it will spread to the lymph nodes and blood.
- TB is an AIDS opportunistic infection. Because of AIDS, the number of TB cases has increased. Doctors who treat a person infected with HIV should also test for TB. TB can be treated and cured, even if the patient has AIDS.

How HIV Is Prevented

Although AIDS is not curable, being infected with HIV is preventable. Knowledge is the first defense against infection. AIDS research is ongoing. New findings constantly update and change what is known about AIDS and HIV infection. It is vital, then, to be alert to new information as it becomes available.

Facts about AIDS and HIV infection can be obtained from a variety of sources. Newspapers, magazines, and health news on television and radio often report the latest scientific findings. The CDC as well as many state and local health organizations are excellent resources for accurate information about AIDS and HIV infection. On a personal level, teachers, school counselors, church leaders, and doctors can either be sources themselves or provide guidance about where to find information.

Despite knowing the possible consequences, some people continue to participate in behaviors known to increase the risk of HIV infection. The following actions will lessen risk of infection during sexual intercourse, but not eliminate it:

- Abstaining from sexual intercourse and intravenous drug use.
- Selecting a sexual partner who is not infected with HIV.
- Having only one sex partner.
- Using condoms correctly. (Condoms are not 100 percent effective in preventing infection with the AIDS virus. According to the Alan Guttmacher Institute, failure rates for average use are about 16 percent.)

HEALTH UPDATE

LOOKING AT THE ISSUES

Having HIV and a Baby

Even with a one-in-three chance of passing HIV to her baby, some HIV-infected females are choosing to become pregnant. An infected baby could get very sick and die in only a few years.

Analyzing Different Viewpoints

ONE VIEW. These women are dying. They want to leave a part of them behind. It's their right to do as they wish.

A SECOND VIEW. Persons infected with HIV often feel very alone. Having a child to love and be loved by would provide emotional strength in their final days.

A THIRD VIEW. Having a baby under these conditions is very selfish. These women will not be around to rear any of their children. If a baby does become infected, he or she will suffer greatly. Finding a home for a baby that is infected with HIV is very difficult.

Exploring Your Views

1. What is your opinion about these women?
2. How would you advise a female infected with HIV who wanted to become pregnant?
3. If you were older, would you be willing to care for a baby infected with HIV? Why or why not?

LESSON 1 REVIEW

Reviewing Facts and Vocabulary

1. What is AIDS?
2. What is the function of T helper cells?
3. Explain the ways HIV is known to be transmitted.

Thinking Critically

4. **Evaluation.** Do you think an individual infected with HIV is responsible for informing others of the infection? Why or why not?
5. **Synthesis.** Why is AIDS a serious threat to public health?

Applying Health Knowledge

6. Design a poster that tells teens how to avoid HIV infection.

Testing for HIV Infection

LESSON 2 FOCUS

Terms to Use

- ELISA
- Western blot
- Pneumocystis carinii pneumonia (PCP)
- Mycobacterium avium intracellulare (MAI)
- AIDS dementia (di•MEN•chuh) complex

Concepts to Learn

- Two tests detect the presence of HIV antibodies.
- A diagnosis of AIDS is based on several factors.

Presently, testing for HIV is required for people who donate blood, body organs and tissue, and for those who join the armed forces. Testing is recommended for State Department Foreign Service employees and people in the medical profession. It is also recommended for people who have practiced behaviors known to transmit HIV. Because of the stigma associated with HIV infection and AIDS, results of tests for HIV are kept confidential.

Detecting HIV Antibodies

As you know, when a pathogen enters the body, the immune system produces antibodies to fight and destroy the pathogen. The immune system does produce antibodies to fight HIV, but these antibodies are not effective in preventing HIV infection. However, finding these antibodies in the blood indicates a person is infected with HIV.

ELISA and Western Blot

In 1985 the ELISA test was developed to detect the presence of antibodies for HIV. **ELISA** means enzyme-linked immunosorbent assay. ELISA is a test for HIV infection, not a test to determine the disease AIDS. ELISA is used for screening donated blood. ELISA also is used on persons who suspect they are infected with HIV because of behaviors they have chosen. One ELISA is given. If a person tests positive, two more tests are done. If after the three tests, two or three are positive, then the Western blot is done to confirm the test results. The **Western blot** is a more expensive test to use but is very specific in identifying HIV antibodies.

Test Results. A positive test means that the person has HIV antibodies in his or her blood. This person is infected with HIV although he or she may show no signs of the disease. In fact, a person infected with HIV can feel and look fine. However, this individual can still infect others when practicing behaviors known to transmit HIV. A person can be infected with HIV for 10 to 12 years or longer before showing signs of infection. Many people who have the disease AIDS actually became infected with HIV years earlier.

A negative test means that there were no HIV antibodies in the sample of blood. It does not mean, however, that the person is uninfected. After being infected, it may take the body anywhere from two weeks to six months or longer to develop HIV antibodies. If a person concerned about possible exposure to HIV does test negative, he or she should be retested in six months. During that six-month period, behaviors known to transmit HIV must be avoided. If the second test is negative, the person is probably not infected with HIV.

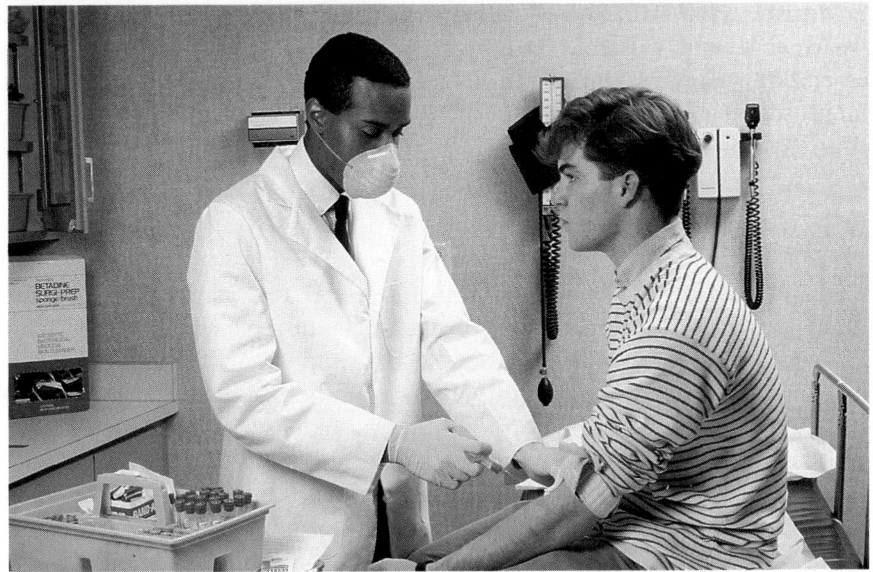

Anyone who has engaged in high-risk behavior should be tested for HIV.

Symptoms of HIV Infection

Although symptoms of HIV infection may not appear for 6 months to 10 to 12 years, a person infected with HIV will eventually develop the disease AIDS. A person infected with HIV will experience many symptoms before a diagnosis of AIDS is made. Symptoms include fever, rash, headache, body aches, swollen glands, and the decreasing ability to fight pathogens. T helper cell count decreases. In a later stage, thrush appears. This fungal infection results in white spots and sores in the mouth and infections on the skin and in mucous membranes.

Diagnosis of AIDS

Diagnosis of AIDS is based on several factors, including a positive test for HIV antibodies and the presence of an opportunistic infection. As mentioned earlier, these illnesses result from a breakdown of the immune system. A person who has been diagnosed with AIDS may live only a few months or for several years. AIDS patients die from the effect of opportunistic infections. Several opportunistic infections are associated with AIDS. **Pneumocystis carinii pneumonia (PCP)** is a form of pneumonia with symptoms that include difficulty in breathing, shortness of breath, fever, and persistent cough. **Mycobacterium avium intracellulare (MAI)** is the leading cause of wasting syndrome, a gradual deterioration of all body functions. It is characterized by fatigue, sudden high fever, severe night sweats, cramps, and weight loss.

AIDS dementia complex is a progressive disorder that destroys brain tissue of a person with AIDS. Symptoms range from mild confusion to inability to control one's muscular movement.

Research and Treatment

There is no cure for HIV infection or AIDS. However, since 1981 the world's scientific community has made great progress in AIDS research.

DID YOU KNOW?

- The effects of AIDS dementia complex are a serious concern for anyone infected with HIV. One-third of those infected with HIV will experience problems with thinking, memory, and coordination. Another third will experience slow, progressive problems. The last third will not be affected.
- Researchers are discovering that the rate of decline of T helper cells seems to be a factor for the development of AIDS dementia complex. Those with rapidly declining rates seem to have the most problems on cognitive tests.

Scientists have gained enough information to develop experimental treatments and possible vaccines. Through concentrated efforts in researching HIV, scientists' understanding of the immune system has increased. It is hoped this knowledge will help advance the fight against this disease.

Medical Research

In March 1987 the medicine zidovudine (AZT) was approved by the Food and Drug Administration for use in treating persons infected with HIV. AZT slows the multiplication of HIV and seems to help delay the onset of opportunistic infections. It also can help reduce the severity of some AIDS symptoms and prolong life. AZT does not cure AIDS. With estimated annual costs of treatment ranging from $2,000 to $4,000 per patient, AZT is an expensive medicine. Almost half of all AIDS patients must stop taking AZT because it damages their bone marrow or because they are infected with a strain of HIV that is naturally resistant to AZT. Other medicines, dideoxyinosine (ddI) and dideoxycytidine (ddC) also have been approved for use to fight HIV. Data on ddI show that this medicine can be used as an alternative and reduce effects of AZT. Some persons taking ddI and ddC have experienced nerve damage to the hands and feet. Effects of taking ddI also include inflammation of the pancreas.

A variety of approaches is being used in an attempt to discover a vaccine against the AIDS virus. A main focus has been finding a protein that will cause the body's immune system to produce effective HIV antibodies. Experimental vaccines have been developed through gene splicing. Only time will tell whether the antibodies produced by the vaccines can protect the body against HIV.

LESSON 2 REVIEW

Reviewing Facts and Vocabulary

1. What determines a diagnosis of the disease AIDS?
2. List two medicines currently being used to treat AIDS.
3. What precautions should a person take whose first test for HIV antibodies is negative?

Thinking Critically

4. **Analysis.** Compare the ELISA and Western blot tests.
5. **Evaluation.** Why do you think the number of AIDS cases continues to increase?

Applying Health Knowledge

6. Develop a one-minute public service announcement (PSA) to inform the public about the serious spread of HIV infection. Submit the PSA to a local radio station and to your school office to be read over the public address system during announcements.
7. Make a list of where people can get information about HIV infection and AIDS in your community.

CHAPTER 9

REVIEW

Reviewing Facts and Vocabulary

1. What is the connection between HIV infection and AIDS?
2. How does HIV attack the body's immune system?
3. Where do lymphocytes move and what function do they serve?
4. What is the function of T helper cells?
5. What happens when T helper cells become infected and are destroyed?
6. Through which body fluids is HIV known to be transmitted?
7. AIDS is not curable, but it is preventable. What are the best methods of prevention?
8. How can using alcohol and illegal drugs increase a person's risk of HIV infection?
9. What role does sexual intercourse play in the spread of HIV?
10. What are the two main tests for detecting HIV? Which is more specific?
11. How long might it take the body to develop antibodies to HIV after being infected?
12. How long can HIV stay in the body before a person shows signs of infection?
13. What does a positive test for HIV mean? a negative test?

Thinking Critically

14. **Evaluation.** Do you think all health care providers should be tested for HIV? Do you think the results should be made known to a provider's patients? Why or why not?
15. **Evaluation.** Why do you think many people are uninformed about HIV infection and AIDS?
16. **Evaluation.** Do you feel that people who are known to have AIDS should be legally banned from entering the United States? Why or why not?
17. **Evaluation.** Do you believe that people should be required to undergo a test for AIDS before being considered for employment? Why or why not?
18. **Evaluation.** How can having sex only in a marital relationship minimize the risk of contracting AIDS?
19. **Synthesis.** Your friend has been engaging in behaviors that could lead to HIV infection. He has had his blood tested for HIV antibodies, and the result has been negative. What should he do next?

Applying Health Knowledge

20. Your friend Sam will be undergoing surgery in a few months that will require several blood transfusions. How much risk does Sam run because of this? How can Sam minimize the risk of receiving blood contaminated with HIV?
21. Why is confidentiality an important aspect of HIV testing?

Beyond the Classroom

22. **Community Involvement.** Interview five people in your neighborhood. Ask them what they think are the five primary causes of infection with HIV. Are their ideas based on fact or fiction?
23. **Further Study.** At the present time, AIDS is an incurable disease. Many diseases of the past were also incurable until medical researchers found a way to combat them. Choose one of the following diseases and write a report on its history: polio; tuberculosis; pneumonia; bubonic plague; malaria.
24. **Community Involvement.** Find out what organizations in your communtiy are helping people with AIDS. Make a list of these organizations and tell what specific steps each is taking to help AIDS patients.

Glossary

A

Abortion. The termination of a pregnancy.

Abstinence. Deciding not to have sexual intercourse.

Acquired immune deficiency syndrome (AIDS). A fatal communicable disease with no effective treatment or known cure. The final stage of infection caused by the human immunodeficiency virus (HIV).

AIDS dementia complex. A progressive disorder that destroys brain tissue of a person with AIDS. Symptoms range from mild confusion to inability to control one's muscular movement.

Amniocentesis. A procedure used to reveal chromosomal abnormalities and certain metabolic disorders in the fetus. The test is done after the 16th week of pregnancy.

Amnion. A fluid-filled sac around the embryo; also called bag of waters. This sac acts like a shock absorber, providing a moist cushion that protects the embryo.

Antibodies. Proteins that help destroy pathogens that enter th e body.

B

Birth defects. Include defects present at birth, including genetic conditions or problems caused by environmental factors.

Birthing centers. Home-like settings available in some hospitals. There the female can have her baby with her family present if she wishes.

Blastocyst. What the cells are called when a cavity forms in the center of a zygote.

Blended family. A family that is formed when two adults marry and have children from a previous marriage or marriages living with them.

C

Cesarean birth. A method of childbirth in which a surgical incision is made through the abdominal wall and uterus. The baby is lifted out through this opening.

Cervix. The neck of the uterus.

Chlamydia. The most common STD. It is caused by several different microorganisms that are similar to bacteria. Chlamydia attacks the male and female reproductive organs.

Commitment. An agreement or a pledge to do something in the future.

Communication. The exchange of information between or among people.

Condom. A thin sheath of latex or animal tissue that is placed on the erect penis to catch semen.

Conflict. A strong disagreement or opposition between persons. Con-flict can happen in any relationship.

Contraception. Preventing pregnancy. Methods of contraception, or birth control, can be divided into nonprescription and prescription.

D

Developmental task. Something that needs to occur during a particular age period for a person to continue his or her growth toward becoming a healthy, mature adult.

Diaphragm. A soft rubber cup with a flexible rim that is worn inside the vagina. The cup covers the cervix.

E

ELISA. Enzyme-linked immunosorbent assay. ELISA is a test for HIV infection. It is used for screening donated blood and on persons who suspect they are infected with HIV because of behaviors they have chosen.

Embryo. The implanted blastocyst.

Endocrine system. A body system that works closely with the nervous system in regulating body functions and is made up of ductless (tubeless) glands that secrete chemicals called hormones.

Epididymis. A highly coiled structure located on the back side of each of the testes. It stores newly produced sperm.

Episiotomy. An incision to open the skin between the vagina and anus to prevent it from tearing.

Estrogen. A sex hormone produced by the ovaries.

F

Fallopian tubes. Tubes on each side of the uterus. They receive an ovum from an ovary. Fertilization of the ovum usually occurs in the widest part of the Fallopian tube.

Fetal alcohol syndrome. A condition of physical, mental, and behavioral abnormalities and birth defects that results when females drink alcohol during pregnancy.

Fetus. The developing baby from the eighth week until birth.

G

Genital warts. Also called venereal warts. Genital warts are transmitted only sexually and are highly contagious.

Genital warts may be caused by a number of different viruses.

Goal setting. Making decisions that will help you meet a goal you have in mind.

Gonads. A term used to describe the reproductive organs, specifically the testes in the male and the ovaries in the female.

Gonorrhea. An STD caused by a bacteria that live in warm, moist areas of the body. This bacteria specifically attacks mucous membranes of the penis, vagina, rectum, or throat.

H

Heredity. Genetic characteristics passed from parent to child.

Herpes simplex virus (HSV). An STD with symptoms of blisterlike bumps that begin 2 to 20 days after contact with the virus.

Homosexuality. The state of being homosexual, or having a sexual preference for someone of the same sex.

Hormones. Substances that regulate the activities of different body cells.

Human immunodeficiency virus (HIV). The virus that causes AIDS. When HIV enters the body, it attacks the immune system.

I

Incest. Any sexual activity between family members who cannot marry by law. It can involve fathers, stepfathers, mothers, stepmothers, uncles, aunts, brothers, sisters, or any relative. It usually involves persuasion—an adult using his or her power and influence on a child.

L

Lymphocytes. White blood cells made in bone marrow. They move throughout your lymphatic system between blood and lymph tissue and help your body fight pathogens.

M

Masturbation. Touching one's own genitals for sexual pleasure.

Menstruation. When the lining of the uterus breaks down and passes through the vagina and out of the body. The menstrual period usually lasts 4 to 7 days.

Mycobacterium avium intracellulare (MAI). An opportunistic infection associated with AIDS. MAI is the leading cause of wasting syndrome, a gradual deterioration of all body functions.

N

Natural family planning (NFP). The rhythm method; a method of contraception that involves determining the fertile days of the female's menstrual cycle.

Nongonococcal urethritis (NGU). An STD caused by several different kinds of bacterialike organisms that infect the urethra in males and the cervix in females. Most cases are caused by the chlamydia pathogen.

O

Oral contraceptives. Oral birth control pills. They contain hormones that work the same way as the natural female hormones—estrogen and progesterone.

Ovaries. The female sex glands situated on both sides of the uterus. They house the ova and produce the female sex hormones estrogen and progesterone.

Ovulation. When one ovary releases one mature ovum into that ovary's Fallopian tube.

P

Pelvic inflammatory disease (PID). A painful infection of the Fallopian tubes, ovaries, or both. PID can result in sterility in both the male and female.

Penis. A tubelike organ that functions in sexual reproduction, pleasure, and elimination of body wastes.

Personal identity. The factors you believe make up the unique you.

Pituitary gland. The master gland of the endocrine system. Its hormones regulate the growth rate and influence the action of the other glands.

Placenta. A structure that forms along the lining of the uterus as the embryo implants. The placenta serves as lungs, liver, kidneys, endocrine glands, and digestive system for the developing embryo.

Pneumocystis carinii pneumonia (PCP). An opportunistic infection associated with AIDS. A form of pneumonia with symptoms that include difficulty in breathing, shortness of breath, fever, and persistent cough.

Postpartum period. The period of time from the birth of the baby until a female begins her menstrual period again.

Progesterone. A sex hormone produced by the ovaries.

Puberty. The period of growth from physical childhood to physical adulthood—a time when an individual becomes capable of reproduction.

Pubic lice. Parasites also known as crabs. They are crablike insects that infect pubic hair and feed on human blood.

R

Rape. Sexual intercourse through force or threat of force. Rape is illegal. It is not an act of passion; it is an act of violence.

S

Scabies. Tiny parasitic mites that burrow in the skin. They are not always acquired by sexual contact. Close bodily contact is a common way to transmit them.

Scrotum. A sac that holds the testes in outside the body.

Self-concept. The mental image you have about yourself.

Semen. The mixture of sperm and fluids from the seminal vesicles, prostate glands, and Cowper's glands.

Sexual response cycle. A series of sexual responses, which are similar for males and females. The sexual response cycle includes the excitement, plateau, orgasmic, and resolution phases.

Sexuality. Refers to everything about you as a male or female person.

Sexually transmitted diseases (STDs). Diseases that spread from person to person through sexual contact.

Sperm cell. The male cell that unites with an ovum to form a fertilized ovum.

Spermicide. A chemical that kills sperm that come into contact with it.

Sterilization. A surgical procedure that makes a male or female incapable of reproducing.

Syphilis. An STD caused by a bacterium called a spirochete. Symptoms of syphilis develop in stages.

T

Testes. The male sex glands.

Testosterone. The sex hormone produced by the testes.

U

Ultrasound. A test that uses intermittent high-frequency sound waves to make pictures of the body's inner organs by recording their echoes. This test can be done early in the pregnancy and can be done several times throughout the pregnancy to check the baby's position as well as the position of the placenta.

Umbilical cord. The structure that connects the embryo to the placenta.

Urethra. A tubelike organ that travels through the penis.

Uterus. A very strong, elastic muscle, about the size of a fist. The primary function of the uterus is to hold and nourish the developing embryo and fetus.

V

Vagina. A very elastic, tubelike passageway, about four to five inches long. Also called the birth canal.

Vaginitis. An inflammation of the vagina. It is a very common condition and affects most females at some time.

Value. A principle that is important to you.

Vas deferens. Connects the epididymis with the urethra. A tube that sperm travel in.

Vulva. The external organs of the female reproductive system. They consist of the clitoris, mons pubis, labia majora (outer lips), labia minora (inner lips), and the vaginal opening.

W

Western blot. A more expensive test than ELISA but very specific in identifying HIV antibodies.

Withdrawal. When the male removes the penis from the vagina before releasing semen.

Z

Zygote. A fertilized ovum.

Index